The Lyric Wore Lycra

A Liturgical Mystery

by Mark Schweizer

Liturgical Mysteries
by Mark Schweizer

Why do people keep dying in the little town of St. Germaine, North Carolina? It's hard to say. Maybe there's something in the water. Whatever the reason, it certainly has *nothing* to do with St. Barnabas Episcopal Church!

Murder in the choirloft. A choir-director detective. They're not what you expect...they're even funnier!

The Alto Wore Tweed
The Baritone Wore Chiffon
The Tenor Wore Tapshoes
The Soprano Wore Falsettos
The Bass Wore Scales
The Mezzo Wore Mink
The Diva Wore Diamonds
The Organist Wore Pumps
The Countertenor Wore Garlic
The Christmas Cantata
The Treble Wore Trouble
The Cantor Wore Crinolines
The Maestro Wore Mohair
The Lyric Wore Lycra

**ALL the books now available at
your favorite mystery bookseller or sjmpbooks.com.**

"It's like Mitford meets Jurassic Park, only without the wisteria and the dinosaurs..."

Advance Praise for *The Lyric Wore Lycra*

"As a writer, Dr. Schweizer is clearly at the top of the bell curve."
Dr. Richard Shephard, retired Headmaster

"Instead of judging whether this book is good or bad, we should be like, so what, can't we all be brothers?"
Chris Tinkler, actor

"This is a book that celebrates inclusiveness, commitment, and the love God has for all people, regardless of intelligence or literary taste."
Sherry Carter, professional Easter bonnet judge

"Not using this book for your church's Lenten Bible Study would be like celebrating the feast of St. Ictis without the weasels."
Susan Messersmith, trumpet player

"I'm coming back from the future to write this review and let everyone know that you can buy this book in 2047 for only twenty-seven cents. Totally worth it!"
Carson Reed (age 2)

"I just love how Schweizer doesn't care how he comes across. He has the boldness of a much better writer."
Stacey Lindsay, retired banker

"Best Cambodian cook book I've ever read!"
Pam Stone, comedian, actress, and author

"This book is pretty good, but not as good as the movie in my head."
Beverly Easterling, soprano and incidental character

"If you're ever just reading along, and you discover that you're reading a 'book within a book,' just hold on sister, because you're in for the ride of your life!"
Jay Goree, lead singer for The Carburetors

"Schweizer is an author obviously not burdened with an overabundance of schooling."
Dr. Robert Lehman, church musician

"I'm sorry, I can't get past the title."
Beth Brand, ghost-writer

The Lyric Wore Lycra
A Liturgical Mystery
Copyright ©2017 by Mark Schweizer

Illustrations by Jim Hunt
www.jimhuntillustration.com

All rights reserved. No part of this publication may be reproduced, stored in a retrieval system or transmitted in any form or by any means electronic, mechanical, photocopying, recording or otherwise, without the prior written permission of the publisher.

Published by
SJMPBOOKS
www.sjmpbooks.com
P.O. Box 249
Tryon, NC 28782

ISBN 978-1-5323-4152-6

July, 2017

Acknowledgements
John and Karen Dixon, Beverly Easterling, Robert Lehman,
Donis Schweizer, Chris Schweizer

Prelude

"It's just too much," said Pete. "Where is it written that the father has to be there for the delivery? Remember the good old days when fathers loitered in the waiting room, smoking cigars, and telling that joke about the rabbi, the priest, and the minister?"

"I agree," said Cynthia. "Well, not about fathers, and that joke is not one bit funny, but I agree with your general contention. That birthing room is a circus. I just poked my head in. There's a video camera set up in the corner, a photographer with a zoom lens lurking uncomfortably close, the "birth-sister" is blogging, and there are Instagram photos being posted every few minutes by someone named Keera."

"Oh," said Nancy, "that's just the Cybergram Digiographer that someone gave them as a baby shower present."

"Someone?" said Pete, giving Nancy a sideways look.

"Well," said Nancy with a grin, "Dave helped too." She shrugged. "She already had enough swaddling clothes, Pete. Get into the twenty-first century."

Cynthia looked down at her watch. "It's been an hour. I guess the obstetrician is in there too, but who knows what *he's* doing?"

"He's tweeting," said Noylene, hearing a ding, and looking down at her phone. "Everything going well. Just a few more minutes. hashtag: #firstbabyoftheyear."

"Are you kidding?" said Pete. "Hashtag? That baby oughta be named Hashtag."

Pete Moss was sitting on an uncomfortable vinyl bench, rolling a cigar around in his fingers as if getting up the nerve to light up. He wouldn't though, and we knew he wouldn't. He'd already been thrown out of more than one hospital waiting room. Cynthia Johnsson, the mayor of St. Germaine, was up and pacing. Noylene Fabergé Dupont, the local beautician and professional waitress, had kicked back in a vinyl chair, one of three that matched the bench where Pete reclined — standard hospital waiting room furniture, aluminum tubing supporting just enough padding to make it uncomfortable, but not unbearable; red vinyl to hide the bloodstains.

Dave Vance was occupying one of the other chairs, and hadn't said anything for quite a while, having his head buried in a *Garden and Gun* magazine he'd picked up off the coffee table. Now he looked up.

"Did you know that a .22 mag can take down a deer at a hundred yards?" he said. "I'm thinking about trading in my .30-06."

"Good plan, Dave," said Pete with a snort. "While you're at it, trade in your pistol for a slingshot."

"I don't have a pistol," said Dave, then thought a moment. "Today is Tuesday, right? Nancy has the pistol."

"The St. Germaine Police Department only has one pistol?" asked Pete.

"Two," said Nancy. "Mine and Hayden's. Dave doesn't need one."

"And Hayden's is in the organ bench at the church," said Dave.

"Still," said Pete, "it seems like you guys should have more than two pistols. What if there's a terrorist attack, or a shootout, or something?"

"That's a salient point," said Nancy. "We do have multiple assault rifles, some stun grenades, and a rocket launcher back at the station."

"Really?" asked Pete, perking up.

"No."

"Hey, Chief," said Dave, looking at me, then pointing down the hall to the delivery room. "Why aren't you in there with the rest of them? I'm sure I saw your name on the birthing invitation."

"All of our names were on the birthing invitation," said Cynthia. "I just can't bring myself to go in. It sounds like a party in there."

"I don't think they're going to miss me right now," I said. "I'll go in just in time to see the big event."

"Do you think that's wise?" asked Cynthia. "You could be in a lot of trouble if you miss it."

"I'll take my chances. I'm watching the Twitter feed. Besides, it's too loud in there to think. I'm mulling over my new story." I flipped my notepad in his direction.

"So what's your title?" asked Pete. "*The Singers Wore Satin?*"

"Not sure just yet. Something with velour perhaps, or maybe moleskin. It'll come to me."

"Tweeting," said Noylene. "Down the chute #miracleofbirth."

"Chief! Chief!" came a familiar voice from down the hall. I looked up from my letter and saw Pauli-Girl McCollough in the hall. Pauli-

Girl was a nurse aid at the hospital and still working her shift, but she'd come over to the obstetrics ward as soon as she'd seen the tweets.

"Coming," I called down the hall, then got to my feet and said, "it's time," to no one in particular, probably to myself.

"Yes, it's time," agreed Pete, and stood up with me. "You're going to need moral support."

"Oh, for heaven's sake," said Cynthia, taking the lead down the hallway. "What a couple of babies! Let's get going."

"Do you really think that Meg's comfortable with all those people in there? She has quite a job to do," said Nancy, following along. Dave and Noylene brought up the rear.

"Not my call," I said. "I know when to stay out of things."

"Not Meg's call either," said Cynthia.

"She hasn't ever done this before," I said.

"How hard could it be?" said Pete. "I mean, women have been doing this very thing for hundreds of years, if I'm not mistaken."

Cynthia glared at him. "You'd do well to shut up from this point forward," she warned him.

She got to the door first and peeked in. The rest of us looked in over her shoulder. The party atmosphere had settled down to a hushed expectation and the onlookers already in the room were staring intently and holding their collective breaths. I looked at Meg. She was breathing and puffing in a rhythmic cadence just as she was taught in childbirth class. I know this because she made me practice with her regularly. Her hands were tightly clasped in the hands of her birth partner.

Pete pushed me from behind, and Cynthia made the room for me to squeeze in. It was small, too small for twenty or so gawkers, but comfortable as all these rooms tend to be. It was a hospital room, sure, but with quilts, and low lighting, and a decor that might have seemed at home at the Grove Park Inn. Even the bed had a homey, arts and crafts look, though the bottom rail had dropped and the doc had pulled up a stool, getting ready to play catcher.

There was a stifled grunt of agony mixed with tremendous exertion. Not a scream exactly, but what wanted to be a scream, cut short in deference to the crowd, no doubt.

"Here she comes," said the doctor. "Somebody tweet that for me. I'm kinda busy here." He seemed to snatch the baby up and out in one motion, although I was sure there was more to it than that. The nurse had the newborn wrapped and lying on her mother's chest in another moment, a knitted cap on her tiny head.

"You did it!" whispered Burt Coley. "You really did it, Tiff!"

"And you're a father," said Tiff, looking relaxed but exhausted. "Say hello to Charlene Micah Coley."

"Heck of a job, coach," said the doctor, reaching over and shaking Meg's hand. Meg, if anything, looked more tired than Tiff. But she smiled widely, looked at me, and gave me a big wink.

"Okay," said the nurse on duty. "Everyone out but the father. Visiting hours tomorrow."

"Are you open tomorrow?" asked Dave, looking at his watch. "I mean today. It's New Year's Day."

"We're open every day," said the nurse, not bothering to look at who would ask so ludicrous a question, as she began rearranging the bedclothes.

"First baby of the new year, I think" said the doctor, tossing his latex gloves, paper gown, and various other items into the waste disposal can. "That's a lucky baby. She gets free diapers, if I'm not mistaken."

"Really?" said Tiff.

"You can check the website," said the doctor, smiling.

The crowd left, one at a time, quietly, and only after placing a hand on the new child. It was like the departing chorus of *Amahl and the Night Visitors*, but without the singing. Finally, Meg stood and she and I took our leave.

Outside, Pete and Cynthia, Nancy and Dave, were waiting for us. Noylene had already headed for home.

"How about a big slice of pie?" said Pete. "It's just two in the morning."

"Sounds good to me," said Dave, then turned to Nancy. "How about you?"

Nancy Parsky was still wearing her uniform since she hadn't been off duty since yesterday, coming straight to the hospital when her shift was over. Tan slacks and shirt, black stripe down the pant, badge, gun belt, sunglasses in the top pocket, lined black leather jacket. Dave was in his uniform, too, such as it was: khakis and a blue button-down shirt. He did have the wherewithal to bring his parka with him. It was cold out.

"Sure," Nancy said.

"I could go for pie," Cynthia said.

"Absolutely," agreed Meg. "I am completely worn out, but I couldn't sleep a wink."

"Lycra," I said.

"What?" said Nancy. "Are you hallucinating? Maybe sleep deprivation?"

"He's probably *free associating*," said Pete. "That's how geniuses work."

"Ah, yes," said Meg. "My husband, the genius. Now I remember."

"It needs to be Lycra," I said again, then pulled my notepad out of my pocket and jotted it down. *The Lyric Wore Lycra.*

"It has a certain flair," said Cynthia.

I just smiled as we headed to the Slab Café in search of pie.

Chapter 1

I sat, listening to the Fauré *Requiem*, reflecting on my very existence as one does when listening to the Fauré *Requiem*. I loved Fauré's *Requiem* as a callow youth, but as I "matured" in my musical tastes, I dismissed it for many years, choosing instead the settings of Mozart, Verdi, and Duruflé, of Brahms and Britten: even Penderecki and Ligeti. All wonderful, of course, but now, it seemed, I had come full circle. Now it was my favorite.

No, I wasn't dying. But I *was* getting older.

And Lent was upon us.

It was the earliest Lent that I could remember, Ash Wednesday being February 6th, just a week away. Theoretically, Ash Wednesday might fall as early as February 4th, but this last happened in 1818 and wouldn't happen again until the year 2285. This fact, I had to look up.

I listened to the baritone soloist begin the *Libera me*. I liked a big voice on this one, and the soloist here was just a little too effete for my taste. Still ... the music ...

Ash Wednesday is always predicated on Easter — forty-six days earlier, to be exact — and Easter, as everyone who is anyone knows, is the first Sunday after the first full moon following the vernal equinox. You can puzzle this out, or you can just look at your calendar. There are forty days of Lent, true enough, but we don't count Sundays. Why? I don't know. I thought about looking this one up, too, but couldn't be bothered when I was distracted by a YouTube video of a priest giving communion on a hoverboard. I watched the whole thing, praying for the hoverboard to explode, but it never did. Sometimes, it seems, God just does not answer prayer.

"What're you doing?" came a voice from the kitchen.

"Brooding over mortality salience and wallowing in unabashed genius," I called back. "It's almost Lent."

"Your genius or someone else's?"

"Not mine."

"You want a beer?"

I frowned. "No, dear, it's ten in the morning."

"But it's Saturday."

"No, thanks," I said. The chorus came in, echoing the opening theme, filling the room with sound. Meg walked into the living room and plopped down beside me on the couch, *plop* being the operative word since Meg was nine months pregnant and due to deliver in a couple of weeks.

"Fauré's *Requiem*, huh?" she said.

I nodded.

Meg had a cup of yogurt in her hand, some mysterious curd from an organic food store. Not regular yogurt, but weird stuff that she now feasted on regularly.

"What are you eating today?" I asked.

Meg held up the cup and read the label. "This one is called Zabadi. It's made from the fermented milk of Egyptian water buffalos."

"And is it good?"

"Meh. I've had better. I thought about getting one made from dog milk, but I decided against it."

"I agree. No dog milk yogurt in this house."

"I'm going to check on the chickens."

"They're fine."

"I still want to check."

"Be careful then," I said. "Don't fall on the ice."

The Requiem turned the corner into the *In Paradisum*. D minor to D major, angels leading us to paradise. Meg disappeared and I got up and went over to my writing desk.

Bad prose was my genre, awful sentences my métier. Now, after years of refutation, I realized this and embraced it willingly, cheerfully, one might even say passionately. This typewriter — Raymond Chandler's typewriter, on which he had penned his first four detective novels — had been instrumental in some of the best and some of the worst detective fiction ever written: both ends of the spectrum.

If you look at a photograph of Raymond Chandler, you see a solemn man, composed, no-nonsense, a pipe unfailingly in his mouth or hand. He was bookish, educated in England in classical literature, then studied international law in France and Germany, before returning to Britain and embarking on a literary career that produced, early on, mostly book reviews and bad poetry.

He came to America on a one-way ticket in 1912 at the age of twenty-four and labored at a variety of jobs, including stints as a tennis racket stringer and bookkeeper for a creamery in Los Angeles. By the time he had married his beloved Cissy, eighteen years his senior, he was on the payroll of a Southern California oil syndicate, and despite his distaste for business, he rose to the position of vice-president. However, as pressures intensified during the Depression, Chandler commenced drinking heavily. In 1932, he was fired from his job.

It was then he turned back to writing, and in 1933 saw his first short story published in *Black Mask*, the most famous of the "pulp magazines." In 1939 his first novel, *The Big Sleep*, hit bookstore shelves and the crime novel would never be the same.

"Chandler wrote as if pain hurt and life mattered," wrote one reviewer.

Chandler was more poetic: *He was a windblown blossom of some 200 pounds with freckled teeth and the mellow voice of a circus barker.*

If you look at a photograph of me, you see the face of a convivial, entertaining individual, mildly sardonic, with more than a hint of devilry. This is what Meg says. I see an old guy going gray. An old guy who can really write.

There was a clue here somewhere, but I couldn't put my finger on it. It kept gnawing away at my brain like one of those praise choruses with only one verse, repeating the same words over and over until you either gave your life to Jesus or killed the woman sitting next to you, the one who kept poking you in the eye with her Tammy Faye Study Bible.

My reviewers are less kind than Chandler's and consist chiefly of the choir members I deem privileged enough to read my stories. For example: "It has been said that great books are lighthouses erected in the great sea of time. This one, however, is more like a dead, vaguely luminescent squid."

I'd been busy for a month or so, but now I felt the muse calling. It was time for the typewriter's occasional foray into the realm of misplaced adjectives, split infinitives, overused modifiers, and all the other horrific abominations that English teachers dream about at night when the grammar goblins begin to call. I took a piece of paper and rolled it gently behind the worn platen, then cracked my knuckles in just the way I imagined Mr. Chandler did it before starting a new story, and leapt into the deep pit of the narrative with no actual idea as to where I was going, who was going with me, or even if I'd make it out with my dangling participles intact.

* * *

The Lyric Wore Lycra
Chapter One

This tale ends as all good crime stories do: the case is solved, the detective makes it with the shapely dame, the jaded but ultimately soapy sidekick finds love in a bottle, the hero gets a new shirt — but here at the beginning, it is exactly opposite, well, not exactly opposite, but pretty opposite.

* * *

Good, good. I could feel the muse tugging at my pronoun agreements. Mr. Fauré's magnum opus had ended and I turned now to Pink Martini, a group touted as "a musically sumptuous and semi-ironic throwback to the faded glossy world of the international lounge orchestra." I didn't disagree. It was great music to write to, or as we professionals say in the literary world, "great music for to which to write." I don't know why we say that. It makes no sense. I popped the carriage return arm a couple of times and placed my fingers back on the keys just the way old Miss Ruddell taught us back in the eighth grade: ASDF—JKL; thumbs up, pinkies at the alert.

* * *

I was sitting at my favorite haunt sucking suds through a tin whistle and poking at the Bubble and Squeak in front of me with the business end of a roscoe. True to its moniker, the food squeaked. I didn't much care for the dish, the English equivalent of Maus mit Nudlen, but it was the Tuesday special at Buxtehooter's and I was a sucker for a deal. Times were hard and the lizard was lean.

"Your supper is squeaking," said the aforementioned shapely dame, a real looker with gams till Tuesday who plopped down across from me and introduced herself as Tryxee Gale, professional soprano, announced her IQ as 180, then proceeded to flounce her intellect all over the table, knocking over the hot sauce.

* * *

Nice, I thought. That's real good writin'. I was kicking metaphors like they were the main attraction at the New Year's Eve Possum Drop.

* * *

"That dish is not quite done," I muttered, firing off a shot, showing the entrée the Big Sleep. "Pass me that hot sauce, will ya?"

"You got noodles all over my decoupage," complained Tryxee, taking a tissue to the front of her Lycra tube-top, a garment so tight and cut so low that orphaned baby cows had taken to following her around the town. "Now I gotta blot my decoupage."

"You mean décolletage, honey," said the beer fräulein, appearing with a couple of refills. She banged them down on the table. "Two more Summer Polecats. That'll be six bits. And honey, you got some stray mouse there on your bosomy parts."

"Eww," said Tryxee.

"You gotta put it on my tab, Erms," I said. "You already got my last coin. I'm busted."

"So what else is new?" said Ermentrüde.

* * *

I heard the slap of the kitchen screen door closing, then the bang of the wooden door, set against the twenty degree temperatures that were common in St. Germaine this time of year.

"It's freezing out there," called Meg from the kitchen, "and it's starting to snow again."

"Hmm," I answered, still engrossed in tightening up a wayward simile or two.

"The chickens are still laying," said Meg, walking into the living room. "I collected a dozen eggs today. The heated henhouse is paying off."

"Never a doubt."

"I was thinking," said Meg, "while I was rooting around under various hens, that since you're working on a new masterpiece, we should have a dramatic reading during the Mardi Gras party at church."

"An excellent idea," I agreed. "Is Charlton Heston available?"

"No, he is dead."

"Really? How about Clint Eastwood?"

"Well," said Meg thoughtfully, "he's not dead, but he's pretty old."

"Patrick Stewart?"

"That's a fine choice," said Meg. "I'll give him a call right after lunch. Now, about this party ..."

"I'm not on any kind of planning committee, am I? I have quite a lot of police work piling up on my desk."

"Really?" It wasn't as much a question as a sarcastic allegation.

* * *

Admittedly, as police chief in St. Germaine, I work less hard than most law enforcement officers in the state. We do have our fair share of murderous goings-on, but the day-to-day police work is principally handled by Nancy and Dave. I view myself as sort of a beneficial overseer utilizing my detecting expertise when required.

Here's the thing: I don't *have* to work at all. I could go ahead and retire. I'm rich. Filthy rich! Meg says, "comfortably well-heeled," but once you've lived in a North Carolina ranger's cabin with three other guys, subsisting on Ramen noodles and squirrel meat for a year or two, a few million is pretty sweet. I do like being the chief of police, though. It has a certain cache, and I've been doing it for twenty-three years.

St. Germaine is a picturesque little town up in the Appalachian Mountains, northwestern North Carolina, not too far from Boone. You might find it on a summer's day, just driving around the mountains enjoying the roadside waterfalls, the unending vistas, the mountain laurel and occasional black bear. You'd see wildflowers, rock formations from the Ordovician Period (a mere 480 million years ago), rivers and rills, and enough beautiful scenery to fill several postcard racks. You'd drive down Old Chambers Road, a serpentine blacktop that doesn't get a lot of traffic since the highway went in about forty years ago, and when you turned that last sharp corner by Dr. Ken's Gun Emporium, you'd pass the Piggly Wiggly and find yourself right smack downtown, driving around the town square surrounding a lovely park. Yes, St. Germaine is a hidden gem in the hollers.

Besides being the police chief, I'm also the organist and choirmaster at St. Barnabas Episcopal church. It's the downtown church, the first church in the community, having been founded way back in 1842. The church had burned twice since then, but has been restored to its former glory and then some. During the past twenty-three years, St. Barnabas Church has enjoyed the ministries of quite a few clergy and staff, good and not-so-good. Priests come and go with regularity. Currently, our rector is the Rev. Dr. Jim Hook who has been with us since Advent.

* * *

"About this party," continued Meg. "We're having a planning meeting on Monday morning at the Slab. Can you make it?"

"I'm always there anyway," I said.

"I'm off to the Pig," she said, heading for the kitchen door. "We need some milk and I'm making a stew that should last us a few days. I'm taking the truck."

"Drive carefully," I called as I heard the door open. "Don't break my truck. And I've changed my mind about that dog yogurt. See if you can find some." But it was too late, the door had slammed.

I turned back to the typewriter.

* * *

"You gotta put it on my tab, Erms," I said. "You already got my last coin. I'm busted."

"So what else is new?" said Ermentrüde, adjusting a wayward strap of her overwrought dirndl and scooping the barley pops off the table and back into her arms.

"I thought sure this was my decoupage," said Tryxee, dabbing at her flotsam and scrunching up her pretty face, pretending she was one of those dames that tossed off three-syllable words like the used tissues that were starting to pile up around her ankles. "You know, I just had my IQ done by one of them Hair Associates at the Walmart. Hair and IQ, only twenty clams."

"Twenty clams well spent," I muttered. "A buck a point."

"No, honey, that ain't your decoupage," said Ermentrüde with a smile so weary it was trying to crawl off her face and take a nap behind her ear. She turned back to me. "The Big Schlemiel says no more credit to you deadbeat gumshoes."

She gestured over her shoulder and I took a look around. Erms was right, the place looked like an out-of-work snooper's convention. It was dark, it was stormy, it was a little after ten, and this whole setup struck a chord: the beginning of a bad novel, part of a song, or maybe a limerick about a man named McSweeny who spilled some gin. Didn't matter. I couldn't remember.

I saw Stink-Eye Lewis sitting by himself at the bar sawing at a plateful of old brogans with a dull steak knife, not even being able to spring a Roosevelt for the gravy. Jimmy Snap was at a table poking at something with his fork that might be shepherd's pie if the shepherd was blind, starving, and had a death wish. C. W. Malooney, Jr. skipped the supper menu and headed straight for the hooch, sucking on an old bottle of rubbing alcohol, a lime stuck to the rim with a piece of Dentyne. Even Rex, the famous detecting dog, was snuffling around a rathole, hoping to find some wayward clergy.

"Times are hard," I muttered again.

"Don't worry about it," Tryxee sniggled, rummaging in her handbag. She came up a minute later with a fist full of sawbucks. "I got cash. Plenty of cash! Now all I need is a detective ..."

The bar suddenly came to life like that dead guy who came back to life in the Bible that time, Lazarus, or maybe Geppetto. Business cards flew through the air, fluttering leaves falling from the shamus tree in the autumn of the shoofly. I swatted them away, quick as they came in, damn shooflies.

"That's right poetic," said C. W. Malooney, Jr. "Autumn of the Shoofly. Can I use that in my memoirs?"

"No," I growled, snapping at Rex, who was the closest. "I'm writing my own memoirs. Now back off, you buzzards. She's all mine."

* * *

A good start.

Chapter 2

"Well, it's about time," said Marjorie, always the first singer to arrive in the choir loft on Sunday morning. She picked up her psalm setting, flipped it over, and began reading my newest detective story printed on the back.

I was at the organ practicing the postlude for the morning, Jean-Joseph Mouret's *Fanfare-Rondeau*, better known as the old theme to Masterpiece Theater.

"*The Lyric Wore Lycra*, eh?" said Marjorie as I reached the final chords. "Well, I guess we all saw this coming. You just ran out of voices."

"I didn't run out," I said defensively. "Lyric is certainly a voice. Well, a voice type."

"Can't argue with that," agreed Marjorie. "I used to be a lyric soprano way back when." She got a wistful, faraway look in her eyes.

"No, you didn't," said Mark Wells, having entered the choir loft and finding his seat in the bass section. "You were an alto with severely impaired high notes."

"I was *not!*" said Marjorie. "Anyway, you weren't even in the choir back then."

"You'll be in the bass section soon," said Mark. "You're already dropping past the tenor range."

It was true enough. Marjorie might have started in the soprano section sixty years ago but, as the years went on, she moved down to alto, then tenor. Now, firmly in her eighties, even the tenor line was getting to be a bit of a stretch.

"I'm *not* singing bass," said Marjorie. "I don't have the time to learn the parts. All those lecher lines ..."

"Just move your lips then," said Mark. "That's what I do. Especially on that Latin stuff."

The choir at St. Barnabas has about twenty-two members, give or take, but we are currently down several attendees due to various circumstances. Rhiza Walker, our best soprano, was in Europe for an extended stay. The word going around town was that she had met someone and he was as rich as the Grand Duke of Luxembourg. The *other* word going around town was that he *was* the Grand Duke of Luxembourg or, at the very least, his younger, handsomer cousin. I had studied music at the same university as Rhiza (although I'd been a grad student when she'd first started) so she was no spring chicken, but make no mistake, Rhiza Walker was still a knockout. I know a good soprano when I see one.

Steve and Sheila DeMoss had been recruited by Father Jim to host a new members gathering that coincidentally met on Sunday mornings during our rehearsal time, so they had begged off till Easter.

Rebecca Watts had the crud.

The other absences were directly related to our "choir-scandal."

Tiff St. James hadn't been back since the birth of little Charlene. Tiff was an alto, our paid scholarship singer from Appalachian State University in nearby Boone. Bert Coley, father of little Charlene, and a deputy with the sheriff's department, had taken a choir-hiatus as well, his from the tenor section.

The two were not married, the principal reason being that Bert already had a wife.

Most of the choir hadn't even known that Tiff might have been seeing anyone until the impending nativity was inadvertently announced in September when it became obvious to Marjorie that *something* was being not-talked-about.

Marjorie: "What's going on? You're getting fat as a bullfrog in summer! Are you pregnant or something?"

Tiff: "Wahhhhhh!"

Even after Tiff's disclosure, she was circumspect about divulging the identity of the father, and Bert stayed well out of the spotlight till the end. It probably wouldn't have affected him professionally, but even at the Watauga County Sheriff's Office, there are more than a few sticklers for traditional family values. As it was, Bert and Heather's newly-filed separation wouldn't result in their divorce for a year, one of the stipulations of a North Carolina decree.

Another choir casualty of the affair was Dr. Ian Burch, PhD, a countertenor anchoring our alto section. Male altos, in North Carolina anyway, are as rare as asparagus in August and Dr. Burch was a good one. Unfortunately he also had the personality of an asparagus. His doctorate was in musicology, his expertise in Medieval instrumental music, his specific interest in the works of Gilles Binchois centering on his oeuvre from the 1430s. This he would tell you through greenish teeth with breath that smelled only slightly better than that of Gilles Binchois himself, a man who had been dead for over five hundred years.

Dr. Ian Burch, PhD enjoyed sitting next to Tiff in the alto section. It was the highlight of his week. When she announced her pregnancy, he was crushed. He held out hope, though, that since Tiff hadn't named the father he might sweep her up and make an honest woman of her, but it was not to be. When he found out that Bert Coley was the progenitor, he departed the choir and no one had seen him since Thanksgiving.

Tiff was gone for now, Bert had departed under a cloud, no one had heard from Ian, and our other tenor, Randy Hatteberg, despised singing duets with Marjorie. You couldn't blame him really, although Marjorie frequently offered him refreshment from the flask she kept in her hymnal rack. Since the tenor section was suffering its own recession, I had taken the opportunity to offer a choir scholarship to a tenor in the ASU Chamber Singers. His name was Bullet.

Bullet was a skinny kid with yellow hair, not the shade of yellow you might see on an actual blond person, but the shade of yellow that adorned South American parrots. It was shaved neatly on the sides, down to the skin, and managed, through some kind of gel-related process, to stand straight up on top. He could sing, though, and had a lovely top A.

"Your name is Bullet?" asked Marjorie, not sure she'd heard correctly.

"Yessam," said Bullet.

"I had a pet rabbit named Bullet once," Marjorie said. "Back in Belgium. Of course, we didn't call him Bullet. We called him Kugel — that was his German name — and we ate him on Palm Sunday. It was after the war, you see. I'd been stationed in France as a nurse, well, that's a whole 'nother story ..."

"You have a last name, Bullet?" interrupted Elaine. Elaine was the keeper of the roles.

"Nope. Just Bullet. Like Beyoncé, or Adele."

"Well, that's interesting," said Phil Camp. The basses had all arrived, Bob Solomon and Fred May completing the section. "How did you come up with Bullet?"

"Well ..." He paused for a long moment, as if deciding whether to divulge the information. "Well," he continued, "my given name is Buster Laverne Titsworth."

"Ah," said Phil. "Enough said."

"Who would do that to a child?" muttered Elaine.

"That's no name for a singer," said Bullet, "so I had it legally changed when I turned eighteen. B-L-T. Bullet."

"Makes sense to me," said Mark Wells. "I always wanted to change my name to Shenandoah."

"You been reading my blog!" yelped Goldi Fawn Birtwhistle, an alto. "Shenandoah is *my* professional name!"

"*Oh Shenandoah, we long to hear you,*" sang the bass section in unison, then broke into laughter.

"It's not funny!" said Goldi Fawn angrily. "You guys shouldn't be reading my blog. It's for my customers."

"We only read it during the announcements," said Fred. "That is, when we don't have one of Hayden's stories."

This was a change for the better, I reasoned. The choir *used* to read my stories during the sermons. Perhaps things were looking up.

"Is your blog for your hairdressing customers," asked Georgia, "or your Christian Astrology customers?"

"My life coaching customers, if you must know."

"You're a life coach?" asked Marty Hatteberg, another alto.

"Well, sure," said Goldi Fawn smugly. "I have five clients. Some of them is crossovers from my astrology business, but they're paying double. I'm a certified life coach."

"Certified by whom?" Georgia Wester wanted to know. Georgia owned the book shop in town.

"Certified by Life Coaches International, LTD," said Goldi Fawn. "I took the whole course. But we're more than life coaches. We're *resilience* coaches."

"As interesting as all this is," I said, "may we look at the anthem for this morning? *The Heavens Are Telling*. It's in your folder."

"There's hardly any season of Epiphany this year," Meg said. "It's almost Lent. I do like this piece. It's nice to sing something uplifting before the lugubriousness sets in."

"You said it," said Marty. "The older I get, the less I like Lent. Oh, I enjoy the parties all right, and Mardi Gras, and king cakes and all, but once Lent squats down and squishes the halleluias out of everything, I'm ready for Easter."

"And that's the point, I suppose," I said.

This chorus, from Franz Joseph Haydn's oratorio, *The Creation*, doesn't have an introduction, but jumps right into the action after a tenor recitative. Since we were skipping the recitative, I gave the pitches, gave a nod, and we were off. Along with the chorus, this anthem featured three soloists. Holly Swofford, Lena Carver, and Bob Solomon handled the trio sections nicely.

Conducting from the console on this one is right nigh impossible. The choir is on their own. I've got enough to worry about. This anthem, though, was a warhorse firmly ensconced in our repertoire and, as depleted as the choir was, I thought we sounded good.

"Nice job," I said, once we'd wrapped up the final cadence. "Now, let's go through Psalm 62 please."

"What's this on the back of the page?" asked Bullet.

"A work of genius," said Bev Greene. Bev had been, in her years at St. Barnabas, Senior Warden, Junior Warden, and Parish Administrator. Now she was content to sing in the choir.

"Genius is sort of a stretch," said Meg.

"Do we sing it?" asked Bullet.

"My Lord, no," said Bev. "At least I hope not."

* * *

The church service went off without a hitch, something new in our experience. When he had arrived in late November, Father Jim Hook managed the services deftly and reverently. He'd been ill after Christmas, but our go-to supply priest was Father Tony Brown, and he was great. Kimberly Walnut, our deacon and Christian Formation Director, had departed last fall and hadn't yet been replaced. We were looking for an associate priest to take up her slack, but for the time being, the temporary position of Children's Ministries Coordinator was being held down by Baylee Trimble, a young mother in the congregation. Her husband, Axel, who had suffered a PTSD episode just a few months ago, was doing fine and was back at his job as a high school principal. Jared, their five-year-old, was now in school, and Baylee had both the time and the energy to devote to the part-time situation.

And so, we celebrated the Third Sunday after the Epiphany, and before long we were enjoying coffee and post-parochial snacks in the parish hall.

Chapter 3

The Slab Café was under attack. Somehow, the word had gone forth throughout the land that the ducks that Pete Moss, the owner of the eatery, had been serving as an entrée (duck and cranberry sandwiches) were the very ones that frequented Sterling Park and were fed and loved by the citizens of St. Germaine.

Never mind that the ducks were a nuisance and that duck excrement slimed the sidewalks, the road, the bandstand, and all the benches in the park. Never mind that these ducks were so fat they could barely waddle, much less fly south for the winter. Never mind that they were happy to hiss and peck at anyone who wasn't tossing bread their way. Never mind that complaints had piled so high at the Police Department that duck grievances now occupied their own shoe box under the counter. Never mind! People were furious. Not the people of St. Germaine, mind you. They'd had enough of the ducks. These people were from Asheville. The Friends-of-Ducks were out in full force on this Monday, eight a.m., the first day the Slab had been open since the story broke in the *St. Germaine Tattler* on Saturday. Six people with placards stapled to yardsticks were marching in front of the café, chanting and quacking on duck calls.

"Duckacide is murder!" chanted one woman. She was wearing an old, olive-drab army jacket, saggy brown leggings, and Birkenstocks, even though there was a foot of snow on the ground. "Quaaaaack!" went her duck call as she pointed it at the front window of the Slab and blew. "Quaaaaack!" came the resounding chorus from the rest of the flock.

"Who are you people?" yelled Pete from inside. It was cold outside, maybe fifteen degrees or so, and he had no desire to mix it up with the Friends-of-Ducks, not in the freezing weather anyway. "You're not even from around here!"

"We're from Asheville, you assassin!" hollered a different woman wearing insulated overalls, a fisherman's sweater, and a thick blue scarf wrapped a few times around her neck. A gray, fuzzy, knit cap covered her head. "It doesn't matter where we're from, murder is murder!"

"You're oppressing the waterfowl!" shouted another demonstrator, this one a thin man with a red stocking cap and a matching scarf. He waved his placard at the window. "Ducks are not sandwiches," was the message.

I waded through the protesters and opened the front door. One of the posters hit me in the back of the head.

I turned to see who did it, not at all amused, and looked into the face of a middle-aged female, brown cap pulled down low, wrinkles abundant on her face. It was the army-jacket and Birkenstock woman. She had a mean look.

"You should be ashamed of yourself," she said.

"Do I know you?"

"No, but I know you. A bourgeois troglodyte. A meat eater." She spat the words at me. "Probably going inside for a duck omelette."

"A troglodyte officer of the law," I said. "So don't hit me again."

"You're not wearing a uniform," said one of the protesters nervously, another man in a worn-out overcoat.

"I don't have to," I said, and flashed my badge at the group. "Stay out here if you must, but if you hit anyone else with a sign, I'll be happy to enforce all your parking tickets."

"We'll gladly go to jail to protect these innocent ducks," said another woman. "Wait ... what? What tickets?"

"Parking tickets," I said. "No sense sending you to jail. You'll just be back here in an hour or two. You are parked illegally, though, and the fine for that is three hundred dollars." I pointed to the cars I assumed were theirs, mostly old junkers lining the streets of the square. Nancy, neatly arrayed in her official uniform complete with leather police-issue jacket, had just finished sticking the last ticket under the wiper of a '74 Pinto. She looked at the group and smiled.

"Three hundred dollars?" said the second man. "No way! That can't be legal."

"Oh, I assure you it is," I said. "We hardly ever give parking tickets since we're happy to have tourists, but once you start attacking police officers ..."

"Apologize, Bonnie," said the man.

"Shut up, Coogan!" said the woman who'd smacked me.

"I can't afford three hundred dollars to save a bunch of ducks," he whispered angrily. "*Apologize!*"

Bonnie bit her bottom lip and said, "I'm sorry for tapping you gently with a lightweight cardboard sign," then added under her breath, "fascist."

I laughed.

"Do we have to leave?" asked the man called Coogan.

"Nah," I said. "I enjoy a good demonstration. Don't tell the owner I said that, though."

"What about the parking tickets?" asked the female protester in the overalls.

"Tell you what," I said as Nancy walked up, "don't hit anyone else, let people come and go as they please, and we'll tear them up at the end of the day. No bothering the customers."

"Okay," said the man.

"Hang on ..." I said, looking hard at the woman called Bonnie. "Are you Bonnie Pickering?"

She looked back at me warily, but didn't answer.

"Bonnie Pickering from Cary?"

No answer.

"Hayden Konig," I said, smiling.

Her eyes flashed but her expression remained unchanged.

"We were in freshman music theory together at Chapel Hill."

Nothing, then, "You have me confused with someone else."

"Ah," I said. "I guess so. Sorry."

Nancy and I went into the Slab and found our usual table at the back. Pete followed us with a full coffee pot.

"They're killing my business," he said, filling our cups.

"No, they're not," said Nancy. "It's freezing outside. No one comes downtown to eat when it's this cold out."

Pete nodded and sighed. "Okay, maybe you're right, but they're not doing me any good."

"They said they'd let your customers come and go without hassling them," I said.

"Ah, the old parking ticket scam," said Pete with a smile. "Glad I thought of that all those years ago."

Pete Moss had been mayor of St. Germaine for many years before he was dethroned by Cynthia Johnsson. Now, being Cynthia's significant other, he preferred to wield his power anonymously behind the scenes. When Pete was mayor, members of the police force could always count on a free breakfast at the Slab Café. It was one of our perks, the other being a free subscription to the *Tattler*. Now that Pete was no longer mayor, we weren't entitled to a free breakfast, but that did not stop us from not paying. Pete had come up with a lot of innovations over the years to increase town revenue, including ultra-expensive parking tickets, and most of them were still on the books. As I said, we very rarely implemented them.

"You guys want a duck sandwich?" asked Pete. "It's the special for one more day. Then, I'm out of duck."

"I don't know if I can eat another one of those sandwiches," said Nancy.

"Especially for breakfast," I said. "I've already had about twelve. It's all you've been serving for two weeks."

"Well, the Sterling Park duck problem is solved," said Pete. "That's the good news. How about duck bacon and eggs?"

"You made duck bacon?" said Nancy.

"It's more like thinly sliced duck between two pieces of toast with cranberry sauce and some Brie. No eggs."

"So, a duck sandwich," sighed Nancy. "Fine. Bring it to me, but this is the last one I'm eating."

"Pancakes for me," I said. "And don't put any duck on them. Just butter and maple syrup."

Pete disappeared into the kitchen.

"Your friend Bonnie was lying," said Nancy, once Pete was gone.

"I know it," I said. "I'm ninety-seven percent sure that's Bonnie Pickering. We went out for about a month during our freshman year. Of course, she's really old-looking now."

"Not like you," said Nancy, taking a sip of her coffee.

The cowbell banged against the glass door of the Slab and Dave Vance came in, saw us at our table in the back, and ambled over, shedding his parka as he walked. Right behind him was Bert Coley.

"Ducks are not sandwiches," Dave said. "I read it somewhere so it must be true."

"I agree," said Nancy, "but it seems we must endure the sandwiching of our web-footed friends for one more day."

"No problem here," said Dave, dropping his coat over the back of the chair and settling in. "I like 'em."

"How are you, Bert?" I said, and motioned for him to join us. "What brings you to town?"

"Job interview," said Bert, sitting down. "You know that me and Tiff are living here in St. Germaine. We're renting a house from Jeff Pigeon up on Laurel Avenue."

"I didn't know that, but I'm not surprised. How's the baby doing?" I didn't ask about Heather.

"She's great." He paused for a moment, then said, "You know Heather moved back to Maryland. She's staying with her parents for now."

I nodded, not knowing what to say to that.

"I feel real bad about the whole thing. I never meant for it to happen. Anyway, Dave told me about a job as a web developer."

"A guy I know from college," said Dave. "He's starting up a company."

"In St. Germaine?" I asked.

"Nah," said Dave, "but web guys can work from anywhere."

"But you're a cop," said Nancy.

"With a master's degree in computer science," said Bert with a laugh. "I liked being a cop, but now I have a daughter and a fiancée who wants to be a stay at home mom."

"I understand," I said.

"I have an interview at Eden Books at nine thirty. The CEO of this new startup called DigiZoot is driving up from Charlotte and stopping by on his way to Kingsport."

"Why the bookstore?" Nancy asked.

"It's the fastest internet connection in town," said Bert.

"I didn't know that," I said.

"Yeah," said Bert. "I don't know why or how, or what Georgia is paying for it, but she has a fiber optic network and she said we could use it this morning."

"Well, good luck with all that. Sit down and have some duck."

"Thanks, I think I'll stick with coffee. I was going to ask ... do you think it would be okay if Tiff and I came back to choir? We miss the singing. Well, and the people."

"Of course! We'll be glad to have you. There's no nursery though. I can set it up if you need one."

"Thanks, but we already have a baby sitter."

"Now back to the woman outside," said Nancy. "Why do you think she disavowed you?"

"Who?" asked Dave.

"Hayden's old girl friend," said Nancy.

"Ninety-seven percent," I said. "I don't know. She saw my badge. Maybe because I'm a police officer."

"And she's an Asheville nutbox," said Nancy. "The ones that are off the grid, they usually don't like to have anything to do with the cops."

"Maybe," I said and looked out on the group. They were bunched together, their placards drooping pathetically. "Maybe I should invite them in for some coffee. It's brutal out there."

"The wind's picking up, that's for sure," said Dave. "Pete's not going to have much business anyway."

I got to my feet, walked across the black and white checkered floor to the door, opened it, and called out, "You guys want to come in and get warm? Maybe have a cup of coffee? There will probably be some customers in an hour or so and you can start back then."

I held the door to the Slab Café open and the wind whistled in. The corner diner on the town square featured several tables covered with red and white checked tablecloths and flanked by wooden chairs. Four booths lined the far wall. Six stools bolted into the floor in front of a long countertop completed the seating arrangements. Salt and pepper shakers, ketchup and mustard bottles, sugar shakers, napkin holders, and a couple of covered cake plates featuring the pie-du-jour made up the decor. Well, those and some Christmas wreaths that were still hanging on the wall, the twenty dollar price tag dangling conspicuously. Noylene Fabergé-Dupont, professional waitress and hairdresser, made and sold the wreaths during the Christmas season. These were the leftovers.

The group of protesters looked at each other, then, without a word, filed into the café one at a time, leaning their soggy signs against the wall by the hat rack.

"This does not mean that we approve of the slaughter," said the thin man with the red scarf. "Or that we even acknowledge your right to make such a horrific decision."

"Of course not," I said. "This isn't even my establishment. I'm sure that Mr. Moss will be happy to listen to your concerns when he comes out of the kitchen. How about some coffee?"

"Where is the wait staff?" asked the woman wearing overalls. The woman I knew as Bonnie had found a seat at a booth and was bunched up in the corner trying to look as inconspicuous as possible.

"Noylene's not here yet," said Nancy. "She's the only waitress. I expect that she's snowed in this morning. The coffee's right over there." She pointed to the coffee maker with three full pots steaming away on the burners. "Just help yourselves."

"I know you," I said, looking at the large woman wearing an old, red North Face parka and one of those red-plaid hunting hats with ear flaps. "You're from St. Germaine, right?"

She nodded, trying to stop her teeth from chattering. "Ellie Darnell. I live up on Highway 194, outside of the city limits, though."

"I've seen you at the courthouse."

"I do real estate title searches. Mostly on-line, but I do need to go to the courthouse sometimes."

"Well, you guys try to warm up."

I went back to our table. The protesters proceeded to drag a table over to the booth and huddle up. We could hear the murmur of their whispered conversation, but since it didn't concern us, we paid them no mind. Dave got up and refilled our cups.

"They certainly don't seem grateful," Bert said, his voice low.

"No, they certainly don't," agreed Nancy.

Pete came out with a duck sandwich and a plate of pancakes, set them in front of Nancy and me and glared at the table by the front window."

"You invited them in, didn't you?" he said.

I shrugged and smiled at him.

"Okay, fine, but all they're getting is pancakes. That's the last of the duck."

"Praise the Lord!" said Nancy, pushing her sandwich in front of Dave. "I'll have the pancakes, then." She purloined my plate a moment later.

"Eat that thing quick, Dave, and we can wrap this up," I said. "These guys can go home feeling like it was a job well done."

"No problem."

Pete walked over to the protesters and spoke loud enough for us to hear. "You've opened my eyes," he said. "I realize now that duck sandwiches are murder and I've seen the error of my ways. We will no longer serve any ducks that were caught in the park."

"There aren't any more ducks, are there?" said the man with the overcoat. "You killed them all."

"That's hard to say," said Pete, contrition in his voice. "I'm pretty sure some of them got away and migrated out of here. Either way, our days of serving duck sandwiches are over."

"What about that one?" asked the woman in overalls. She pointed at Dave who was wolfing down his breakfast.

"That's not duck," lied Pete. "That's chicken — a wild chicken from Tinkler's Knob that willingly sacrificed itself to become part of the circle of life. It ran in front of a school bus. The driver brought it in."

Bert stifled a snort. The protesters all sniffed in disgust.

"Now, how about some pancakes?" Pete said cheerfully. "They're gluten-free!"

After a brief consultation, gluten-free pancakes were decided upon.

"But if we get any word of you serving duck sandwiches again, we will be on you like a horn-worm on a Black Cherokee hybrid!" said Coogan.

"I don't know what that means, but I take your veiled threat," said Pete. He headed back to the kitchen and before we had time to drink another pot of coffee, he was out on the floor serving pancakes to everyone in the place, including two actual customers who had braved the cold and just come in.

"Pancakes are all we have this morning," Pete told the two workmen who were out this cold morning checking on power lines.

"Great!" was the reply.

"I have to say, these gluten-free pancakes are delicious," said the protester with the scarf, wiping the last of the syrup off his lips. "We'll be happy to tell our Asheville friends about your place."

"Since you've decided *not* to kill any more ducks," said another of the group, sternly.

"Absolutely," said Pete. "No more ducks. What a mistake that was. I'm deeply sorry."

"What do we owe you?" asked the first man.

"Call it thirty bucks," said Pete, "and I'll donate it all to St. Germaine Animal Rights.

"Really? Well ... thank you."

"My pleasure," said Pete, smiling.

The half dozen protesters got up, each paid five dollars, retrieved their coats, hats, and still-soggy placards and left the Slab, struggling against the bitter breeze as they made their way to their cars.

Pete came back to our table and slumped down in his chair with a huff.

"Well, was I contrite enough?" he asked.

"Nauseatingly so," said Nancy.

Dave said, "You catch more flies with honey than you do ..."

"Shut up, Dave," said Pete, cutting him off. He stuffed the thirty dollars into his wallet. "Pig food," he muttered leaving us no illusion as to where the cash would end up. Pete's truffle pig would go through thirty dollars in high octane meal in just a few days.

"Hey," said Pete defensively. "I didn't lie. Portia's an animal and she's got rights."

"Indeed she does," I said.

"I gotta say, those pancakes were really good," said Dave.

"And they're gluten-free?" asked Nancy.

"Oh, hell no," said Pete.

Chapter 4

Meg's party planning committee meeting was put off until the afternoon due to the weather, but by two o'clock, the day had warmed to a lovely twenty-nine degrees. Fortunately, I had another obligation, having told the rector that I'd be around to discuss Ash Wednesday and the beginning of Lent. Meg and her party planners were meeting for a late lunch.

Staff and worship meetings at St. Barnabas had been hit or miss for the past couple of months. The new priest had begun his tenure in December, and we'd done really well through Advent and Christmas, but then Father Jim got sick, a bad case of pneumonia that lingered like the stink of a dead woodchuck under the house. After several weeks of being incapacitated, Jim was now managing to do a bit of work at the office and take services on Sunday, but even that left him exhausted.

Kimberly Walnut, our semi-delusional deacon, had been gone since October. Bev Greene, who had been the church administrator, had been fired by the previous priest: Baylee Trimble was brand new on the job and, before long, the worship committee had crumbled into disarray.

This, plus the fact that I found any excuse to miss meetings whenever possible, made those few conclaves we did manage to have fairly productive. No wasted time, no discussing whether it was a good idea to serve communion on stilts, or to give back rubs during the Nicene Creed, or some other ecclesiastical fad du jour. I imagined that eventually the rector would get a grip on all this and tighten the reigns, but for now I didn't complain much. I rehearsed the choir, turned in the music selections to Marilyn who dutifully placed them in the bulletin, played the services, and pretty much enjoyed myself.

"We should go over to the Ginger Cat," said Father Jim. "I didn't have any lunch and the Bear and Brew is closed on Mondays."

"I think the Fat Tuesday planning committee is over there now."

"All the better. They can give us a report when they're done."

"Fine with me," I said.

"Then I have an appointment at Bill the Barber's. That's the new shop on the corner."

"A barber shop that takes appointments?"

"Only on Mondays. Other than that, it's walk-in."

"Feeling any better?" I asked, knowing the answer I'd get. He didn't look any better.

"No. This is really kicking my butt. I'm on another round of antibiotics, but I just have no energy."

The Rev. Dr. James Hook was a priest who had been looking for a nice place to spend the remaining years of his ministry. St. Germaine was perfect for him. He was fifty-nine years old and had served several large parishes, principally in south Florida. He'd taught at a seminary, and had his PhD from Duke University. His wife, Dorothy, had joined us just after Christmas when their house had sold.

When I met Jim last fall, he was tall, lean, and fit. His hair was gray and he was clean shaven, the very picture of a successful Episcopal priest. That was when he came to us in November. Now, he looked ten years older, had a hard time breathing, and coughed often.

We walked over to the Ginger Cat, St. Germaine's fancy eating establishment on the northwest corner of the town square, prime real estate downtown. A block over was the Bear and Brew. Next to the Ginger Cat was Noylene's Beautifery (an Oasis of Beauty), and next to that was Eden Books. The new barber shop was tucked in beside the bookstore. St. Barnabas Church commanded the west side of the square, the courthouse and the police station, the east. The Slab sat diagonally across Sterling Park on the southeast corner. The library and various shops filled in all the available space.

As far as culinary ranking, the Ginger Cat was the highest. The Slab Café might be the lowest on the list, but it was the only place to get breakfast. Also, the Boston Cream pie was delicious. The Bear and Brew was a pizza and beer joint, squarely in the middle: great pizza, great beer. The Ginger Cat, though, had lunch specials like "Squab with warm fois gras sorbet."

"I'll have that," Father Jim said to Wallace, our waiter. "The squab."

"A fine choice," said Wallace. In the tradition of fancy waiters everywhere, Wallace wrote nothing down. "The squab is delicately dressed with a warm foie gras sorbet, beetroot, and cocoa beans, with a protruding leg immersed in Banyuls sauce. The unique taste and flavor blends scrumptiously with the silken foie gras."

"I'll have a liverwurst sandwich," I said. "White bread, some mayo, and a couple of lettuce leaves."

"Would you like a *pickle* with that," said Wallace, contempt exuding from every pore.

"Sure," I said brightly, "and some fries."

Wallace shuddered.

"Oh, just bring him the special," said Meg, suddenly appearing beside my chair, "and pay him no mind, Wallace."

"I don't want to eat a pigeon," I said. "We just got rid of the ducks. Now we have to get rid of the pigeons?"

"Squab," corrected Wallace. "It will interest you to know that we get our squabs at the free-range market in Weaverville. They're not local. They're raised by an organic pigeoner."

"How can a squab be free-range?" I asked. "It will fly away."

"Umm," said Wallace nervously, now realizing that some other patrons were beginning to listen in to the conversation.

"Ignore him," said Meg, pulling out the third chair at the table and sitting. Wallace disappeared gratefully.

"I feel a poem coming on," I said, taking out my notepad.

"He forgot to take our drink order," said Father Jim.

"Just as well," I said. "You would have ended up with a bottle of *Château de Mal Poisson* at a hundred dollars a bottle."

"Nonsense," said Meg. "Bud is recommending a sparkling wine at five dollars a glass."

"Yes," said Wallace, who magically reappeared, immediately realizing his faux pas. "Bud recommends the *Freixenet Cordon Rosado Brut*. The nose is full of cherry and strawberry balanced with a lightly toasted bagel aroma. It is surprisingly dry with a long, fresh finish. Five dollars a glass."

"And it's pink," said Meg.

"Well, if it's pink," I said, "and if Bud recommends it."

Bud McCollough was the eldest of the McCollough children. Moosey was the youngest, now thirteen. Pauli Girl was the middle child, and still in nursing school. Bud had graduated from the university and opened a wine shop in town, I myself being a silent partner. He was a wine savant and had been since he was young, preferring to read about wine and wine culture rather than delving into the world of Harry Potter. When the youngest master sommelier in the country recommends a selection that's "crisp but equally wicked Rhone that kicks you in the butt with hints of bramble, melancholy buttered scones, and the scent of a freshly opened can of tennis balls that will have you convinced you're a poet," customers listen. He'd made a deal with the Ginger Cat, sharing his expertise, and of course, providing the wine at marginally above wholesale prices.

"I'll have that as well," said Father Jim, "and some water, please."

Wallace disappeared again.

"We're just over there," said Meg, nodding toward the table of five other women happily chatting away. "The consensus is to go ahead and have Shrove Tuesday pancakes and the king cakes."

"That sounds just fine," said the rector.

"We'll decorate the parish hall with the traditional Mardi Gras fare," said Meg. "Hayden has agreed to do a dramatic reading of some of his finest prose."

"What?" I said.

"Remember? We talked about it."

"I remember something about Charlton Heston. Nothing about me reading."

"That'll be great," said the rector. "I've heard good things about your finest prose."

"I don't know from whom," Meg said. "It's occasionally funny, but pretty bad. He has won awards for bad writing you know."

"Hey!" I said. "You're the mother of my child. You're supposed to stick up for me."

Meg shrugged.

"How bad is it?" asked Father Jim. "On a scale of Kim Kardashian to William Shakespeare."

Wallace appeared again with warm bread, strawberry butter, and a tray of drinks. "The entrée will be out momentarily," he announced with a flourish of his napkin.

"I'd give it a solid Jackie Collins," Meg said.

"Aw, c'mon," I said, and produced my notepad. "My prose is delightful. For example:

> One morning a free-ranging pigeon
> Accepted a brand new religion.
> He was baptized that day
> in a fois gras sorbet,
> and we dined on him smidgeon by smidgeon.

Nice, eh? Whaddya think?"

"It's okay," said Meg. "Not great. It needs some work."

"How can you say that?" I asked. "It has everything — pathos, religion, humor, and a hint of parsley."

Meg turned to the priest. "The limerick is Hayden's poetic genre of choice. Make no mistake. He won't be doing a reading of his limericks. Not in church, anyway."

"There once was a woman named Meg," I started. "Much admired for the turn of her leg ..."

"That's just about enough of that!" said Meg, standing up. "I'm going back to my meeting. I just thought I'd fill you in on the party."

"Thank you," said Father Jim, as he turned to me. "How does the limerick end?"

"Made the gentleman sit up and beg."

Meg slapped me playfully on the head, and smiled in spite of herself. "Oh, one other thing," she said. "Marilyn said that there are some classes being offered for Lent. We thought we'd have some tables set up in the parish hall with sign up sheets. There's an exercise class, a Bible study, a cooking class. Stuff like that."

"Sounds great," said Father Jim.

Our lunch was served moments later and, as pigeon went, it was a fine repast. We discussed the Ash Wednesday service, the main topic being the location of last year's palm fronds left over from the Palm Sunday processional. These were traditionally burned and used for the ashing of the congregants, a smear of gray-black in the shape of a cross on their foreheads as they repented. Ashes to ashes, dust to dust. Unfortunately, Kimberly Walnut was in charge of keeping the palms for the next Ash Wednesday. In the four or five years she was with us, she never did manage the task, one year even using the ashes of old Lucille Murdock who's family forgot to take her with them after the memorial service. Granted, she was left in a shoebox ...

"Delicious," pronounced Father Jim, dabbing at his mouth with his napkin. "Better than a liverwurst sandwich, eh?"

"I will not admit to that," I said, "but it was good."

"Anything special for the rest of Lent?" he asked. "Different from the usual?"

"We'll switch to the *Kyrie* instead of the *Gloria*. And we'll do *Lamb of God* as the fraction anthem. That is, unless you have another plan."

"Nope."

"Then I think we have everything covered until Holy Week," I said. "We should have another lunch meeting in a month or so."

"Sounds like a plan," said the rector.

Wallace came over to the table and nervously put down the check.

"What's up?" I said looking at him. "You've gone all pale and twitchy. How much is it, anyway?" I reached for the bill, but Father Jim was faster and scooped it up.

"It's on St. Barnabas," he said with a smile. "Worship meeting."

"That's ... that's not ... not it," stammered Wallace. "Lieutenant Parsky said to tell you ..." He paused and the muscles around his mouth twitched.

"Tell me what?" I said.

"There's a woman in a car over by the Slab."

"Yeah?"

"She's dead."

Chapter 5

Is St. Germaine the murder capital of North Carolina? I can say that in the thriving metropolis of Boone, there have been exactly two murders in the last ten years. St. Germaine has managed nineteen in the same span — twenty, if the woman in the car had been done in. Raleigh, in comparison, had one hundred seventy-six. Greensboro, a city half the size of Raleigh — two hundred ninety-one. Percentage-wise we might be slightly higher, but the murder capital? Surely not.

I thought about this as I walked across Sterling Park to where I saw Nancy standing next to an old car in front of the post office. It was the Ford Pinto she'd ticketed earlier, once light blue, now a dingy blue-gray and obviously ready for the junk yard, the principal material in its composition being rust. I was surprised that it had passed the state inspection, but then noticed that it had a South Carolina license plate.

"Good news," she said as I walked up. "It's not your girlfriend."

"Thank heavens for that," I said. "I would have hated it if Meg were the chief suspect."

"It's that woman in the overalls and the fisherman's sweater. The loud one."

"Got a name?"

"I popped the door, made sure she was dead, and went though the glove box. The car is registered to James Witherspoon, but the paperwork is from ten years ago. There's no mention of a Mrs. Witherspoon on any of the registration material and no purse that I can find. I didn't go through her pockets. Not yet."

"Have you called the ambulance?"

"Yep."

I sighed heavily. "Who discovered her?"

"Helen Pigeon," said Nancy. "She was walking by and saw her in the car."

"That's right," said Helen, suddenly appearing beside me. "I was just going to the library and I saw her in the car. I thought she was asleep."

"Helen, I told you to wait in the Slab," growled Nancy.

Helen ignored her. "It's freezing out, so I knocked on the window like this." She demonstrated by rapping her knuckles on the driver's side window. "She didn't move and I could see she wasn't breathing, so I ran over to the police station and got Nancy."

"Thanks, Helen," said Nancy. "Now go wait in the ..."

"I just know it's a murder," said Helen, her excitement evident. "You know, we just started our crime club. The Blueridge Ladies of Murder. This could be our first case."

"A crime club?" I asked.

"Oh, yes! We're going to be known as BLaM." She pointed a gun finger at Nancy and cocked her thumb.

"Technically," Nancy pointed out, "you would be known as BLOM."

Helen waved her hand dismissively. "BLaM. I'm the president, of course, since it was my idea. Then there's Hannah, Amelia, and Grace, you know, the girls from the Piggly Wiggly, and Pammy McNeil and Goldi Fawn."

I did know the girls from the Piggly Wiggly. All three, part-time checkers, all well over eighty, all with concealed carry permits, all packing heat. Pammy and Goldi Fawn didn't have any weapons that I knew of.

"Time to go, Helen," said Nancy, pulling her away from the car and trying to point her back toward the Slab.

"Sure," said Helen. "I already have about a hundred crime photos on my iPhone."

"Helen," I said, "did you or did you not go right over to the police station to get Nancy as soon as you discovered this woman?"

"Well, sure I did, but I had to take some photos first, didn't I?"

"Give me your phone, Helen," Nancy said, her ire still under control, but rising.

"Okay, but I already sent all the photos to the group." Helen smiled innocently.

"Never mind," I said. "Just go wait over in the café, will you?"

"I'll be happy to. Just call me when you need me to testify or do a perp walk or something."

* * *

By the time the ambulance had arrived, there was a small crowd on the sidewalk in front of the Slab. Yes, it was cold, no, there wasn't much to see, but it seems that a dead body is always reason to congregate, speculate, and cogitate.

Nancy whispered, "You think it was a gluten allergy that killed her? If it was, Pete's in hot water."

"I hope not," I answered. "I hadn't even thought of that."

The two EMTs, Mike and Joe, had the woman out of the car and on a stretcher.

"No rigor yet," said Mike. "I'd say she's been dead just a few hours. With the cold and all, maybe five or six?"

"We saw her alive at eight-thirty this morning," I said.

"It's my professional opinion that she expired at some point between then and now."

"That's just great."

"I may be wrong," said Mike, "but I don't think you'll be able to get a more accurate time of death."

"What about checking the ambient air temperature, the temperature of the interior of the car, and the current temp of the victim, then working the numbers?" said a voice behind us. It was Dave.

"Where have you been?" asked Nancy.

"I had a dentist appointment. I just heard about this."

"Well, what about all that?" I asked Mike.

"Might work," agreed Mike, "if the car wasn't out of gas."

"Explain," Nancy said.

"See," said Mike, first pointing at the car ignition which was on, and then the fuel gauge registering E. "I'm thinking she sat here in the warm car, either dead or alive, till the fuel ran out. We don't really know when that was."

"So," I said, "did the carbon monoxide get her?"

"Nope," said Joe.

"How do you know that?" asked Nancy.

"First of all, the car is outside. Granted, this junker may have so many holes in the exhaust system and the floorboards that the fumes leaked through enough to do her in. But it's doubtful."

"Still," I said, "it might have happened."

"Nah," said Joe. "Look here, under her scarf." He moved the material so we could see. "There's some kind of a rubber hose around her neck and it's tied in a knot."

"You guys should be detectives," I said.

"You would have seen it all when she was moved," said Joe, but he smiled in appreciation at the compliment.

"Go ahead and take her down to Kent Murphee. There's no need to go to the hospital."

"Will do," said Joe. "You want to untie the rubber hose and keep it here? Do your forensic thing?"

"No," I said, "leave it where it is. Tell Kent to be careful with it. There might be DNA or a fingerprint or something, but I want to know what he thinks before we go messing with stuff. We'll work on the car till we hear from him."

"I'll let him know," said Mike.

I looked in the back seat of the car. Three books, an empty cloth grocery bag with "Whole Foods" stenciled on the front, an old guitar with no strings, and a baby doll wrapped in a flannel blanket.

Nancy, meanwhile, had been going through the woman's pockets. "Nothing," she announced.

"Figures," I said, then to Dave, "First thing, call the DMV and see if this is her car so we can get an ID."

"Second thing?" asked Nancy.

"Bonnie Pickering, possibly of Asheville, North Carolina. Something's up with her. I can feel it. Anyway, it's a place to start."

***

The Ford Pinto was, or rather had been registered to Buford Witherspoon of Cowpens, South Carolina. According to the DMV, Buford was eighty-two years old, had no insurance on the vehicle, and probably hadn't seen the car for a number of years since the last paperwork available was from 1997. The license plate had been updated with several years worth of forged stickers indicating, to the casual viewer, an ongoing registration. The stickers were homemade, glued on, and covered with some sort of clear finish, fingernail polish maybe. Not a great job, but unless the car was stopped for a violation, there would be no reason to pull it over. Well, except for the fenders falling off. On the back bumper was an old faded bumpersticker advertising Mildred the Bear on Grandfather Mountain and another decal affirming the 1992 presidential qualities of Ross Perot. We searched the car, then Nancy dusted for prints, swabbed for DNA, and had it hauled over to the impound lot in Boone after moving the contents to the police station.

Dave did his usual "people check" doing whatever it was that he did, and found that Buford, or Bubba as he was known, lived at 5846 Culvert Road. Birthday: July 21, 1928. Wife: Fern Lydell Witherspoon, deceased. One daughter, Shirley Camellia Witherspoon, also deceased. He got a phone number and, when he called, ended up talking to a hospice care provider.

"Can I speak with him?" asked Dave, after identifying himself. "It's a police matter."

"You can try."

"How bad is he?" Dave asked.

"Today or tomorrow."

Silence, then coughing on the other end of the line. Dave waited till it stopped.

"Mr. Witherspoon, this is Dave Vance with the St. Germaine Police in North Carolina."

Silence.

"The reason that I'm calling is that a car registered to you — a '74 blue Ford Pinto — has been connected to a murder."

Silence again, then a wheezy voice, "I sold that car twenty years ago to my no-good grandson in Gaffney. Let him have it for three hundred dollars."

"Would that be Shirley's boy?" Dave asked.

"What's he done? Killed somebody?"

"Can you give me his name, Mr. Witherspoon?"

Coughing, then, "No." Click.

"Huh," said Dave, and went back to work, but everything else, including the name of Shirley's son, lead to a dead end.

The information he got on Bonnie Pickering was just about as useful. He found her in Cary, followed her through college, a marriage and a divorce (no children), a move overseas, but back to the states about twelve years ago. She worked at the post office in Mars Hill for five years, then dropped off the radar. She hadn't filed any income tax returns since 2003. She wasn't registered for any government assistance. She had no address, no driver's license, no library card, and her passport had expired the year she came back from living abroad. She was, as we say, off the grid.

"How about the duck people?" I said, hearing Dave's report. "Maybe they know where she is."

"Friends-of-Ducks," said Dave. "Turns out it's not a real organization in the sense of being registered anywhere or with anyone. I called Asheville Voice for Animals. They never heard of Friends-of-Ducks. Neither had the Humane Society or the Animal Liberation Front."

"Animal Liberation Front? Who are they?"

"A militant vegan animal rights activist group. The Humane Society says that they have guns."

"Yikes," I said.

Chapter 6

I led Tryxee Gale discreetly back to my office, no mean trick with those baby cows dogging our steps and bawling like they hadn't had a drink in three days, but I took a few back alleys, then lost them on the fire escape, stupid baby cows.

I ushered her into the back door, made our way down the hall, pushed open the door, and clicked on the light. Someone was sitting in my chair, an unfortunate joe dressed in a bishop suit, complete with robe, pointy hat, and suffragan girdle. He was dead, as dead as a dodo, which was pretty dead, the last sighting being in 1662, the same year that the Bishop of Middle Codswallop invented the suffragan girdle. These coincidences were adding up and I could add, boy could I.

"Oh no," Tryxee sobbed, covering her eyes, but I could see her peeking through her fingers, therefore giving me a clue that she wasn't quite as unzipped as she wanted me to believe. I notice clues like this. It's what I do. I'm a detective. I noticed the baby cow clue, too, but I didn't say anything about it because I wanted it to be a surprise later.

Yeah, I'm a Liturgy Detective, duly sworn in by the diocese, empowered by my life coach, and consecrated into twenty-seven denominations including the Full-Gospel Prediluvians, the Orthodox Anglican Monophysites, and the Lutherans. I had a gun, a badge, a copy of The Watchtower, and a Gideon Bible stuffed in my pants and I wasn't afraid to use any of 'em, especially on those Lutherans.

"Wait a second," said Tryxee. "You've got a life coach?"

I shrugged and gave her a look that said, "Yeah, I've got a life coach, what about it? You've got problems of your own: You're a singer with 67K in student loans, a boyfriend who's run off with your therapist, a 1974 Pinto, a tube-top with the integrity of a dryer sheet, and now you come to me knowing that the bishop you were having an affair with is dead and sitting in my chair." It was a heck of a look and one I'd been saving for just such an occasion.

"How can you look at me like that?" she wailed. "This tube-top is from Target!"

* * *

I picked Nancy up at eight-thirty. We stopped and grabbed some coffee at the Holy Grounds coffee shop just off the square and headed down the mountain. It was another cold day, well below freezing. All the weather reports indicated we were in for a prolonged cold spell. This wasn't unusual up here in the mountains especially in late January. Although St. Germaine wasn't known as a "snow destination" there were plenty of towns around us that were: Beech Mountain, Seven Devils, Sugar Mountain, and they all offered skiing, snowboarding, ice skating, and the like. We did get some overflow into town on the weekends for shopping and eating, but not much. It was frigid, but not snowing and the trip into Boone was easy.

"What are we listening to?" asked Nancy. My pickup had a state-of-the-art sound system and my music collection was extensive.

"*The Passion Oratorio* of Johann Ernst Bach."

"I thought it sounded like Bach."

"Not that Bach," I said. "There were about fifty Bachs running around Germany writing music. This one was Johann Sebastian's nephew I think."

"It sounds like Bach to me. I don't care which one."

"Fair enough," I said.

The good thing about Boone being such a non-murderous town is that, when we do have a gristly killing in St. Germaine, Dr. Kent Murphee, the coroner, is always mighty happy to take some time off from his "middle-aged men dropping dead from heart attacks while shoveling snow" autopsies, and jump into something more interesting.

"This one is nasty," said Kent, puffing on his antique meerschaum pipe. "A two-drink autopsy."

"Kent, all your autopsies are two-drink autopsies," I said.

He brushed a bit of pipe ash off his tweed coat, a garment that hadn't seen a dry-cleaner for thirty years. "Yeah, well ..."

"I'll have my first one now," I said.

"That's the ticket!" said Kent with a smile. "How about you, Officer Parsky?"

"Lieutenant Parsky," I corrected.

"Don't lieutenants go in for plain clothes?" said Kent. "That uniform makes you look like a regular officer."

Nancy shook her head. "I like it. It makes my job easier. And no drink for me, thanks."

Dr. Murphee reached into a desk drawer, came up with a half-empty bottle of bourbon and two short glasses. He poured a couple of fingers into each one. "Nothing like starting early in the day."

"No ice?" I said.

"You are a barbarian," said Kent, and drained his glass in a single gulp, then stood. "Come on, drink up. We don't have all day for you to nurse that thing."

I took a deep breath and downed the bourbon thinking that if nine in the morning was too early to start drinking, it was certainly too early to look at dead bodies.

Kent led us into the autopsy room where the woman was laid out on the table.

"What?" I said. "This isn't the victim, is it?"

"The very same," said Kent.

I looked at Nancy and could see she was as puzzled as I was.

Granted, an autopsy room tends not to present a murdered person in the most flattering way. Lying naked on a metal table, still, pale, bloodless, and generally with some added aberration, a cut throat, or a bullet hole, or something. This woman was a gorgeous redhead and I had to look closely at her face to make sure it was the same woman I'd talked to the day before. Yes, she was still, and yes, she was dead, but she was, or had been, a stunning beauty.

In the past, I might have said something about the deceased's looks that would have been regarded as sexist and probably inappropriate given the circumstances, but Meg had worked her magic on me over the years. Luckily, with Nancy there, I didn't have to.

"Dang!" she said, astonishment in her voice. "She was hot!"

"You are correct" said Kent. "Hot, indeed, but it's not *all* natural. Breast augmentation, very well done. You couldn't tell without close examination. Hair extensions, caps, cheeks, a bit of chin work years ago. Still, the figure is her own, and she kept herself in very good shape."

"We sure couldn't see that under those padded overalls," said Nancy. "Plus, she was wearing a sweater and that gray hat."

"She didn't have any makeup on either," I said.

"She still doesn't," said Kent, "but she's a pale redhead. The blood came to the surface of her face when she was strangled, gave her that rosy glow."

"Never heard of that," I said.

"It's not that rare," said Kent. "There are nonspecific physical signs used to attribute death to asphyxia. These include visceral congestion via dilation of the blood vessels — drowning, essentially. Petechial hemorrhaging, that is, small veins broken by high intravascular pressure. We can spot these in the eye most easily. Then there's cyanosis. As asphyxia progresses and more oxygen is depleted, a discoloration of the skin and tissues called cyanosis develops. In this case, and at present, it presents as a rosy color. Most certainly her face will take on a bluish hue by tomorrow."

"Are you going to open her up?" asked Nancy.

"Not unless you need me to," said Kent. "There's no reason. She was obviously strangled. Death from asphyxiation. Doesn't look like she struggled, though. It just seems like she went to sleep. Well, except for the rubber thing around her neck. Anyway, white female, around forty-five years old, red hair, green eyes, five feet, nine inches tall, one-hundred forty pounds."

"We need to know who she is, Kent," I said. "Can you get a serial number off one of those breast implants?"

"Huh," said Kent, thinking for a moment. "I hadn't thought of that. Well, yes. I'll bet I can."

"Is she pregnant or anything?" asked Nancy.

"She wasn't pregnant," said Kent. "I did all the regular blood work, too. She's clean as a whistle — in perfect health other than the fact that she's dead. She did have a rare blood type: AB-negative. Less than one percent of the population has it."

Nancy and I stood on either side of the cold, metal table and studied the woman in silence for a couple of minutes.

"Here's something you will find interesting," said Kent finally.

Nancy and I looked at him. He was standing by the side table, holding up the murder weapon.

"What is it?" I said.

"This rubber hose," said Kent. "It's a hose, sure enough, and made of latex, but it's constructed to resemble something else. Look here." He brought it over and held it up so we could view it closely. It was a mottled blueish-white color, about three feet long, and had a spiral ridge along its length. "It looks to me like a movie prop. It could be something from a medical supply company, though."

I looked at Nancy. She shrugged.

"I give up," I said. "What is it?"

"It's a human umbilical cord."

* * *

Sure enough, Dr. Murphee found the serial numbers and three hours later we had a name. Sabrina Bodkin.

Chapter 7

"*Who?*" said Meg.

"Sabrina Bodkin," I answered.

Nancy and I had gotten back to town and I met Meg for a late lunch at the Slab. Cynthia, who wasn't scheduled to wait tables today, but was in Pete's office paying the bills, had joined us. Pete was in the kitchen breaking in a new short order cook.

"Oh, my word!" said Meg. "I had no idea it was her. You said it was one of those Asheville animal rights women."

"It was," I said. "You know Sabrina?"

"Yes, and so do you!" said Meg, sounding miffed. "Or you would have if you'd ever paid a bit of attention."

"What on earth are you talking about?" I said.

"She was the woman who taught our childbirth class. The one we took back in October."

"No," I said, thinking back to the class, then to the woman on the table. "I would have remembered this woman, I promise you."

"Red hair, tall, a great figure," Meg said. "She wore black rectangular glasses."

"Sounds right," I said, "but no glasses. Nancy and I went over to the morgue. I'm sure I never met this gal."

"Fiddle faddle," huffed Meg. "You only went once and didn't participate much, as I recall."

"Fiddle faddle?" said Cynthia with a laugh. "Who are you, Jane Austen?"

"I beg to differ," I said, remembering. "The teacher was a middle-aged doula from Lenoir. She had dark, frizzy hair and wore green scrubs. She talked about eating placentas cooked up with acorn squash in an afterbirth stew. She had us hum the *Baby Elephant March* on one breath to get our diaphragms working. We had to do squats. *Squats!*"

"That was only for the first class," said Meg.

"Then she came outside and yelled at me for having a cigar during our break. I was outside, for crying out loud."

Meg rolled her eyes and snipped, "That teacher was a sub. I can't even remember her name." Realization dawned on her face, then, "Ah, well, obviously you should have come to the rest of the classes with me. You would have met the real teacher."

"But sweetheart, I am not your labor coach. You did not want me to be your labor coach. In fact, you told me that under no circumstances was I to be your labor coach."

It was true. Cynthia was Meg's coach. Meg was afraid that I would tell jokes during her labor, even though I had promised that I would try my best not to. I was allowed to be in the room, but no jokes, and if she heard even one, I was to be escorted out by Nancy, presumably in handcuffs.

"Irrelevant," said Meg. "If you loved me, you would have come to the classes."

"Yeah," said Cynthia, supporting Meg as any good coach would.

"And done what? Watch you two pretend to squirt babies out on the floor of the St. Barnabas parlor?"

"Yes," said Meg. "That's exactly what you should have done. That's what the other husbands did, and they did it happily."

"Happily because ...?"

"Happily because they were co-birthing their child, of course," sniffed Meg.

"And," added Cynthia with a smirk, "it had nothing at all to do with the fact that the teacher was a stone cold fox who wore skintight leggings and midriff Lycra tops to demonstrate the birthing positions and breast feeding. As I recall, the other men didn't miss a class."

"Hmm," I said. "An interesting fact that I was not made aware of at the time."

"Well," said Meg, "I shouldn't have had to tell you that to get you to come with me. You should have *wanted* to come on your own accord."

"You're absolutely right of course," I said, knowing that any position I might take was untenable in a nine-month pregnant woman's eyes. I decided to change the subject. "Let me ask you something. Did you guys practice with rubber babies? I mean, *realistic* rubber babies?"

"Sure," said Cynthia. "They were kinda gross. Like they were straight out of the womb, you know what I mean? They looked slimy, but they weren't. Just rubber."

"How about umbilical cords?"

"Yep," said Cynthia. "That was realistic, too. It popped off the baby when you gave it a yank. We stuck it back on for the next class."

"Three feet long, blueish-white, sort of spirally?"

"Yes," said Meg. "Why?"

"Sabrina was strangled with it. The rubber baby was left in the back seat of the car."

"Oh, my God!" said Meg.

"Okay, what would you like for lunch?" asked Pete, walking up to the table. He was dressed in his usual jeans and Hawaiian shirt, this covered with a cardigan sweater in deference to the temperature outside. In his younger days, he would have been in sandals, even in January, but these days he'd switched to boots, just to keep his feet warm, he said.

"I couldn't possibly eat," said Meg. "We just found out that the murdered woman was Sarina Boinkin."

"Sabrina," I said. "Sabrina Bodkin."

"Yes, that's right," said Meg, sadly. "She was the woman who taught our birthing class back in September. Truth be told, she wasn't very professional. Always giving the husbands the come-hither."

"Cynthia told me about her," said Pete. "The hot one? Wow! She's the one who got murdered? I thought it was one of the protesters."

"It was," I said. "She was the loud one in the insulated overalls."

"You're kidding."

"Nope. Now, how about a Reuben sandwich? With fries."

"Me, too," said Cynthia. "Although I am sorry that Sabrina's dead, I'm really sort of hungry."

"Okay," said Meg, "make it three, but I'm still feeling bad about it."

"No reason not to," I said as Pete disappeared back into the kitchen. "Do either of you know if she was still teaching childbirth classes in the area?"

"No idea," said Meg. "I saw her last week over at the church. She was wearing her regular clothes though, not her birth-teaching attire."

"Who would be in charge of that?" I asked. "Scheduling birthing classes, I mean."

"Well, you're on the church staff," said Cynthia. "I presume you would know who's in charge of that stuff."

I sighed heavily. "Okay, maybe Father Jim has a handle on it. My bet is, though, that he doesn't. Maybe Marilyn."

Meg said, "It's great for you as a musician to be left alone to do your job, nobody bugging you, but quite frankly, there's no one watching the henhouse."

"I'm beginning to get that," I said.

* * *

I went over to the church after lunch, principally to talk with Marilyn. I found her at her desk proofreading the upcoming church newsletter.

"You know," she said when she saw me, "this could use some punching up. I mean, how many articles about the food pantry and upcoming Lenten studies can we do?"

"I presume the question is rhetorical."

"It is. How about adding one of your choir mysteries?"

"Nah," I said, "but I can write you a quick Bible study article."

Marilyn eyed me askance.

"It could be a problem though. You may be getting requests for the newsletter from all over the world. *The St. Barnabas Bugle* will go global."

"I think that's a chance we're willing to take. Let's do it."

"When do you need it?" I asked.

"Today."

"Consider it done. You need some kind of permission?" I gestured toward the priest's door.

I'll ask Father Jim if it's okay, but really, he hasn't put a quash on anything since he's been here."

"Nothing?"

"Nothing," said Marilyn. "He's gone this afternoon. Another doctor's appointment I think. Do you need to see him?"

"Nope. I wanted to see you."

"Really? Why?"

"The woman that we found dead in the car over by the Slab ..."

"I heard about that," said Marilyn. "Someone we know?"

"It was the lady who was holding the childbirth classes in the parlor."

"Oh, my God!" said Marilyn, her hand fluttering up to her mouth. "Sabrina?"

I nodded. "I know we let organizations meet in the church. There's AA that meets on Wednesdays, and this childbirth thing. So I was wondering who was in charge of scheduling the building, making sure there aren't any conflicts, vetting the programs, and such."

"Vetting the programs?"

"You know, so the church isn't hosting the Raëlians looking for a meeting room to contact their home planet."

"They do that?" asked Marilyn.

"Most assuredly," I said. "I have it on the best authority."

"Well," said Marilyn, punching up a screen on her computer, "AA has been meeting here since God's dog was a puppy."

"Yep."

"The childbirth class was scheduled by Kimberly Walnut last summer before she ... um ... left us. There were a couple of expecting mothers in the congregation, including Meg. The rest of the class came in from around the area, I suppose."

"Makes sense," I said.

"They used to meet Tuesdays at four, but the class finished up a month ago. The next one wasn't scheduled to start for a few weeks. Sabrina was here last week getting everything scheduled and checking on expectant mothers."

"We should cancel it for now," I said. "Put up a notice or something."

Marilyn made a note, and continued. "Then there's a book club that meets here on Sunday afternoons. Diana Evarts is in charge of that. I think Meg's mom is in it. Diana isn't a member of St. Barnabas, but several church members are in the group, so she came in and talked to Father Jim about that one and he okayed it."

I nodded.

"Then we have some Lenten programs coming up. They start next week."

"Uh huh."

"There's a cooking class being taught by Susan Clark. *Making Scripture Cookies.*"

"Doesn't sound too bad," I said. "And there are cookies at the end."

"Here's one you might be interested in ..." Marilyn gave me an evil smile. "*Lose Forty Pounds the Yah-Way.*"

"Oh," I said.

"That one was scheduled by Baylee. I heard that it's being led by one of her friends over in Boone. I heard that there will be materials and Biblical vitamin supplements available for purchase."

My head dropped.

"You might want to pop in on the second session. *Jesus is My Personal Trainer*."

"You are now toying with me, aren't you?" I said sadly.

"Rodell Pigue and Sammianne Coleman want to host a church-wide meeting on the transgender bathroom issue. Rodell says sooner rather than later."

"What transgender bathroom issue?"

"You know ... the whole transgender bathroom issue."

"I *don't* know," I said. "We don't have an issue. Every one of our bathrooms is a single use facility."

"Well," said Marilyn, "all I know is that Rodell and Sammianne are very concerned." She perused her list. "There's a new exercise class called *Paunches Pilates*. It will meet in one of the Sunday School rooms. The word is that if the class wants to keep it going after Easter, they can do that."

"*Paunches Pilates?*"

"Yep," said Marilyn. "The class on casting out unwanted spirits hasn't been advertised yet. I just got that email this morning."

"What?"

"It's from someone called Shenandoah, forwarded by Father Jim," said Marilyn, and pulled it up on her computer screen.

I read through it quickly. "Time for some meetings," I sighed. "I knew it was too good to be true."

"It's good to have you back," said Marilyn. "You want some coffee?"

Chapter 8

My old '62 Chevy pickup rumbled up the highway toward home at a fair clip. This truck was an antique, but since I was one as well, I was happy to keep it. A year ago I had taken it to a guy who knew a guy who did restorations. I didn't really have it restored, but it looked as though it was. I went for the upgrades though: a new high-tech engine, fancy on-board computer, new suspension, new transmission, leather seats, a state-of-the-art sound system, drive train, and such. The body looked original, but with a new blue and white paint job, a lacquered oak truck bed, new mirrors and chrome. There was even a pistol safe hidden underneath the front seat.

In point of fact, there wasn't much left of the old truck. I didn't mind. With its four-wheel drive, weather did not phase us. It went up and down the mountains in snow, sleet, and rain, and never broke a sweat. The lights would activate in "police mode" and I could pull someone over just by flipping a switch instead of fumbling for my dash light and struggling to plug it in to the cigarette lighter while driving fifty miles an hour.

All this came at a price, almost ten times as much as the truck cost when it was new. Did I mind? I did not.

I drove out of town, up Old Chambers, and headed ten miles into the mountains toward home. Meg and I had a two hundred acre spread on which I'd built a "cabin" when I made my first million. The cabin was actually quite a fine house situated on a river right in the middle of the property. It was home to Baxter the Swiss Mountain Dog; Meg; me; an owl named Archimedes; a trio of owlets, Winken, Blinken and Nod; six chickens, unnamed in case we decided to eat them; two goats that grazed freely and did have names once, now long-forgotten; and a plethora of wild animals that inhabited the woods and riverbank nearby. I'd thought about getting a cat at one point, just to keep the mice at bay, but Baxter did not like cats.

In late January, the landscape in the mountains of North Carolina is austere, bleak, mostly made up of grays, browns, and a few dark greens — grays rendered by the rock formations that framed every bend in the road and jutted from the hills at startling angles; browns by the floor of rotting leaves, tree trunks, and vines that managed to scrabble some nourishment from what was very harsh and lithic terrain. The mountain laurel and rhododendron were evergreens, but their leaves took on a darker hue in winter. Green, yes, but a melancholy green, green waiting for something to happen. Pines and firs dotted the landscape but, in the dead of winter, everything seemed quieter, more somber. The pine trees didn't sing like they did in the spring and summer. That's what Meg said, and she was right.

A selection of Palestrina masses was on the stereo, the current offering being the *Missa Brevis*. As far as Renaissance vocal music goes, Mr. Palestrina's compositions for the church are the pinnacle. The title is slightly misleading as *Missa Brevis* generally denotes a short mass, but this one is not *brevis* in the least. It is about twenty-five minutes of pure genius. Vaughan Williams once said that the *Benedictus* from this exquisite work was the most perfect music he had ever heard. I couldn't argue. Twenty-five minutes is just about exactly the time I need to get home and the *Agnus Dei* finished up just as I drove up to the garage beside the house. Baxter was outside to meet me. He was a large dog with a distinctive tricolored coat, black with white chest and rust colored markings above the eyes, sides of mouth, front of legs, and a small amount around his white chest. There was a white "Swiss cross" on his chest. He was eight years old and we braced ourselves against the realization that he didn't have many years left. Seven to eight years was the life expectancy of his breed, but Baxter was active and healthy and showed no signs of slowing down. He barked twice in greeting then took off toward the back of the house where his dog door was located.

Meg was not home, a fact I realized when I opened the garage door and saw no sign of her Lexus. I parked the truck, got a *Headless Heron Pumpkin Spice Ale* out of the beer fridge in the garage and walked across the yard to the house. Baxter was in the living room when I got there, lying in front of the cold fireplace waiting for someone, anyone, to set fire to the logs and make his life complete. I was happy to make it happen.

I opened my beer, then settled in behind my typewriter, reread my manuscript in an effort to maintain some sort of expository thread, then decided, the heck with it and jumped right in.

* * *

"So, you're a singer," I said, deciding to try my luck at conversation since eye contact wasn't working.

"I'm a lyric soprano," breathed Tryxee breathlessly. "I started out as a dramatic, then I went to soubrette, then spinto, then lyric-spinto, then coloratura, then dramatic-bel canto, but now my coach says I'm a lyric."

"It's good to know your fach," I said, wondering just how one would pack a hundred and forty pounds of pork sausage into a Lycra tube the diameter of a garden hose.

"Exactly!" said Tryxee. "That's it. My fach!"

I peeled my eyes away and looked outside — the rain was cascading down the greasy window, beading up like that time you used Turtle Wax on your car before you realized it was made from real turtles: not that you had a love for anonymous turtles and this was before "environmental consciousness" was a thing, but your pet turtle, Shelton, wouldn't ever look you in the eye again.

"It's you I want," she panted, flinging herself onto the davenport, like one might fling a sausage onto a davenport.

* * *

I took a sip of my beer and contemplated the narrative. If this wasn't genius, it was the next thing to it. I heard Meg come into the kitchen.

"Hey, there," she called. "I'm home. Is Baxter inside?"

"He's by the fireplace warming up," I called back. "I'm in here working on my *opus maximus*. C'mon in here and see what you think."

* * *

"Save it, Cupcake." It wasn't that I was not untempted, but rather that I was not nondisposed to the uninveiglement. I smiled ... a sextuple negative, maybe a new record.

"What?" she said, batting her big blue eyes like Carl Yastrzemski in the '67 World Series, if the opposing pitcher was throwing eyeballs instead of baseballs. "What's uninveiglement?"

My gaze narrowed. "Hang on ... are you reading my thought bubbles?"

"Sure!" she glittered. "It's one of my talents." She produced a piece of foolscap from a discreet crevice. "Lookit, I have a list."

I poured myself a shot of rye.

"Tryxee's talents," she read. "Written by Tryxee, copyright by Tryxee, all rights reserved by Tryxee.

Number 1: Singing."

I snorked.

"Number 2: Caring, maybe too much.

Number 3: Reading thought bubbles.

Number 4: ... "

She looked up at me and tittered bouncily. "Well, I think Number 4 is obvious." She gave her shoulders a shake and the whole davenport collapsed under the resulting tremor, 7.8 on the Richter scale. She gave a little coo and continued.

"Number 5: Walking on the beach at sunset.

Number 6: ... "

"That's plenty," I growzled. "Unless Number 6 is 'furniture repair,' I've heard enough. Now what's your game, sister?"

She pulled me down onto the floor and kissed me like I hadn't been smooched since that time I ended up with a mouth full of suckers playing Spin-the-Octopus with the finalists of the Miss Cephalopod beauty contest.

"This is the game," she whispered.

"Spin-the-Octopus?" I gasped.

"No," she slurped. "The game of love ... "

* * *

"Spin-the-Octopus?" said Meg. "Have you ever played Spin-the-Octopus?"

"Not personally, but I have it on great authority that it's the teen party game of the future."

"What happens when your daughter wants to have a party over here and asks you to pick up the octopi?"

"That's when she goes to the convent. The Little Sisters of Adversity and Discipline swoop in when she's asleep and whisk her off in the middle of the night. We'll get her back when she's twenty-five. I've already contacted them and she has a standing reservation."

"Hmm," said Meg, "I'm not saying it's a bad idea, but let's keep it in reserve."

"From everyone I've talked to, it's the only way we'll be able to survive. You forget how old we'll be by that time."

"I know. What were we thinking?"

"Nothing for it now," I said, taking a sip from my bottle. "Would you like a beer?"

"I'm having a baby in two weeks!"

"So, I'm guessing, no?"

Meg harrumphed and went back to the kitchen, Baxter trailing behind her.

Chapter 9

The crime club, or BLaM as they wanted to be known, was in full operation when I came into the Slab the next morning. We, that is, the St. Germaine Police Department, had been having our morning meetings at the Slab Café since Pete Moss was mayor and we had a designated table in the back. That is to say that our table was sometimes occupied, especially during peak tourist season, and on those occasions we would go elsewhere — Holy Grounds Coffee Shop for instance, or maybe the Bun in the Oven bakery. Generally, though, we could be found at the Slab from eight until nine fifteen on most mornings. We felt it was important to be available to the community and, if anyone had a crime to report between eight and nine fifteen, this is where they could find us. No one ever had. Crime it seemed, in St. Germaine at least, could wait until a decent hour, or until we'd had our coffee. I saw Nancy and Dave parked at our table, coffee already poured.

The Blueridge Ladies of Murder had pulled two four-tops into the middle of the room, and commandeered seven of the chairs. Helen Pigeon was sitting at the end. She had a notebook, a cup of coffee, several pens, and a pair of handcuffs on the table in front of her. Hannah, Amelia, and Grace sat on one side of the tables, Pammy McNeil, Goldi Fawn Birtwhistle, and Kimmy Jo Jameson on the other. I did a double-take when I saw Kimmy Jo. The last time I saw her was a few years ago when she judged the St. Germaine Christmas parade. She was the widow of NASCAR driver, Junior Jameson, now buried in Wormy Acres inside his race car.

"Hi, Kimmy Jo," I said. "How have you been?"

"Real good," she said, her low-country drawl matching her big Southern smile. "It's good to see you, Hayden."

Kimmy Jo had big blonde hair and a figure close to Barbie proportions that she obviously worked very hard at. Her makeup was a tad too much, her teeth a tad too white, her hair a tad too high, her drawl a tad too slow. It was a cultivated persona and one that, in my opinion, was fostered by a certain type of woman, professional athletes' wives for example, at least for a time.

"Are you back in town? I see you've hooked up with this august crime fighting group."

"Kimmy Jo moved back last week," said Helen. "She's got her real estate license and she's taking over Jeff's brother's office."

"Jes' part-time," said Kimmy Jo. "I don't want to work full-time. You know that Junior-Junior and Ashleigh are still in high school. I'm also starting an exercise class over at the church."

"I think I heard about that," I said.

"Yep. *Paunches Pilates*," said Kimmy Jo. She gave me another smile. "It's going to be coed. Men welcome."

"I'll certainly think about it," I said, having no intention at all of thinking about it.

"All the girls are signing up, aren't you, girls?"

There were some grudging nods around the table, then Hannah said, "Are we gonna need our Berettas?" She looked warily around the café. "Because we got 'em in the car."

"Nope," I said. "You won't need them." The three octogenarians peered at me through narrowed eyes.

"We got carry permits," said Amelia.

"You won't need them," I reiterated. "Truly."

"I brought mine anyway," said Grace. "You never know." She pulled out her handgun and laid it on the table. A Beretta .38 caliber automatic — a lightweight pistol that packed quite a punch.

"Okay, then," I said. "Here's the deal. Do not take out your guns for any reason whatsoever. Grace, you put that thing away."

Grace made a face and slid the gun into her purse and out of sight.

"I don't even have a gun," said Pammy.

"Good," I said.

"I have a shotgun," said Goldi Fawn.

"We *all* got shotguns," said Hannah. "What you need is something you can carry around in your purse."

"You could saw it off, prob'ly," offered Amelia. "Keep it in your coat pocket."

"Don't saw it off," I said.

"Do you have any intel for us?" asked Helen. "We need the coroner's report, and we'd like to see the Murder Book. We already have all the crime scene photos."

"Murder book?"

"We read that you coppers always keep a Murder Book that has all the clues and evidence and stuff in it."

"Well, we don't, and if we did, I don't think that you ..."

"Freedom of Information Act!" Goldi Fawn blurted out, as if answering a game show question.

"That's right," said Amelia and banged a fist on the checkered tablecloth. "Freedom of Information Act! And the Second Amendment!"

All seven women glared at me. I didn't even know where to start with this one so I said, "Well, you got me. As soon as we start our Murder Book, you'll be the first ones to see it."

The women at the table nodded and smiled and Helen wrote something on her pad.

"Let me know if you find the perp," I said, and headed back to a table in the corner.

"We've got our own handcuffs," said Helen. "Now, ladies, let us open with a prayer ..."

***

Dave, Nancy and I were in the middle of our high-level meeting concerning whether country ham should be added to the four major food groups when Dave's phone rang. He excused himself and moved to the next table to talk.

Nancy said, "Police work, I guess."

"Pass me that last biscuit, will you?" I said. "And the sawmill gravy."

"That was Angelique at the post office," Dave said, once he'd hung up and rejoined the meeting. "Hey! Where's my biscuit?"

"It was here just a second ago," said Nancy.

"Anyway," said Dave, still surveying the table in case that biscuit was hiding behind a ketchup bottle or something, "Angelique says that she knew Bonnie Pickering."

"Really?" said Nancy and I in unison, my voice muffled by half a mouthful of gravy-dipped, buttered goodness.

"Post office employees," said Dave, "especially in the little towns around here, comprise a small club. They stay put and might work their entire careers in the same place. Bonnie Pickering worked for five years in Mars Hill. Angelique remembers her. Says she would see her at employee events."

"Good work," I said. "How does that help us?"

"I dunno," said Dave. "Just thought it was worth checking on. Now, can I get another biscuit, or what?" This last comment was directed at Noylene, the only waitress working the breakfast shift.

"Sure, hon," she said. "You want some apple butter?"

"Just gravy thanks," Dave said. "Maybe some more coffee?"

"Coming up," said Noylene, then disappeared into the kitchen.

"Did you ask Angelique if she's heard from Bonnie since she quit?" Nancy asked.

"Of course I did," said Dave, "and no, she hasn't."

"How about Christy?"

"I didn't ask Christy."

"Next stop," I said, "the post office. After breakfast, of course."

"Should we tell the crime club?" asked Nancy with a smirk. "They might need this information."

Noylene reappeared with a biscuit slathered in light brown gravy and a coffee pot. Sawmill gravy, at least the way it's served up at the Slab Café, is a coronary infarction waiting to happen — milk, an abundance of black pepper, some flour, and thick with spicy ground sausage.

"Do any of y'all want one of them Christmas wreaths on the wall?" said Noylene, putting the plate in front of Dave. "I'm reducing the price to just eight dollars."

We looked up at the wall. There were six wreaths left including one of her signature "Santa at the Manger" wreaths that featured two main characters: Santa on his knees, praying, and the baby Jesus looking up from his manger with startled eyes. Festooned with hot-glue around the wreath were various animals also ostensibly visiting the newborn babe — mostly the traditional barnyard animals, but also a sprinkling of meerkats, armadillos, and a penguin or two that Noylene had found on sale at the Atlanta Zoo. The infant Jesus was played in this wreath-o-rama by a small plastic Japanese baby in a kimono.

The other five wreaths were decorated with birds, fruit, feathers, fantastic animals, and whatever else struck Noylene's artistic eye at the moment of creation.

"I'll give you five dollars for that one with the rats in top hats eating candy canes," said Dave.

"Them's mice," said Noylene, squinting at it. "At least I think they are. Seven fifty, that's my rock-bottom price. You sure you don't want that Santa at the Manger? It's a beauty. There's ten dollars worth of animals not even including Santa and Jesus."

"I'll take the rat one," said Dave, fishing out his wallet.

"I'll have it wrapped and waiting for you at the register," said Noylene with a smile.

* * *

Georgia Wester was in front of me in the line at the post office, if you could call one person a line.

"Morning, Hayden," she said. "Catch the bad guys yet?"

"Nope," I said. "Speaking of bad guys, it's time for a worship committee meeting. Aren't you still the Senior Warden?"

"This week," said Georgia, warily. "What's up?"

"General stuff," I said. "The church is hosting several Lenten classes including *Paunches Pilates, Lose Forty Pounds the Yah-Way, Scripture Cookies Made Easy,* a seminar on casting out unwanted spirits led by Goldi Fawn Birtwhistle, and I have it on good authority that the Raëlians will be using the four-year-old Sunday School room to try to contact their home planet."

"What? You're joking!"

"Only about the Raëlians."

"WHAT?"

"It's our fault really," I said. "Father Jim showed up in Advent, but all the services and activities had been planned for months, then Christmas just took care of itself. The Altar Guild had its job and did it. Same with the lay readers, servers, ushers ... no problem."

Georgia looked disgusted.

"Then Jim got sick, Epiphany came along, and here we are a month later."

"Meeting tomorrow!" said Georgia angrily. "I'll get Marilyn to set it up." She turned to Angelique who was at the counter and growled, "Gimme a book of those stupid 'Love' Valentine's Day stamps."

"See you tomorrow," I said cheerfully.

"Cripes!"

"She seems stressed," said Angelique, watching Georgia exit the building.

"Yeah."

"Are you here to ask about Bonnie Pickering? I already talked to Dave."

"Just a few questions, if that's okay."

"Sure," she said. "Fire away."

"You knew Bonnie from Mars Hill?"

"Well, I knew her when she *worked* over in Mars Hill. I'd see her at a Christmas party, or when we had a post office event we had to go to. She came up here and subbed once or twice. She was sweet. Quiet, but not shy, y'know? We hiked together a few times."

"Do you remember anything she talked about that might let us know where she is?"

Angelique shook her head. "Christy might know more than me. They were sort of friends, at least for a while."

"Is Christy here?"

"Today's her day off."

I looked out the front plate-glass of the post office. From where I was standing I just might have been able to see Sabrina's car if I looked past all the flyers and ads that folks had taped to the window. "You guys didn't see anything Monday morning? Maybe that old Pinto parked in front?"

"Nope," said Angelique. "Well, there were some cars out front parked across the street when we got here, but I didn't notice much about them. Then they drove off. The only people that came in were Pete and Cynthia, and that was later. It was a cold one. We were here all morning. Never left."

"Can you give me Christy's phone number?"

"Sure," said Angelique. She pulled her phone out of her pocket, scrolled through it and held it up so I could see. I wrote the number down, thanked her, and headed for the office.

* * *

I called on the way into the office, but Christy didn't answer her phone. Nancy and Dave were both there and working when I arrived.

"Nothing new from Angelique, except that Christy might have some more information. She knew Bonnie Pickering better than Angelique did."

"So, where are we?" asked Nancy.

"Well," I said, scratching at my head, "let's go over it. We have a dead woman named Sabrina Bodkin. She was strangled with a rubber umbilical cord, most certainly pilfered from her back seat. No one walks around with an umbilical cord in their pocket."

"Strangulation is usually a man's purview," said Nancy. "Gotta have a lot of muscle behind it."

"What if she was already knocked out?" asked Dave. "Then anyone could have done it."

"I agree," I said. "Especially with that rubber cord. It was thick and it stretched a good deal. Pull it tight and give it a couple of turns and it will do the job on its own. Still, I think you're right. The odds favor a male killer."

I continued. "Kent did the blood work. He didn't find anything out of the ordinary. No knockout drops, no drugs."

"It happened right out in the open," said Nancy. "In a car, granted, but in broad daylight. Okay, it was freezing, and the streets were empty. The few folks that were out were hustling to get inside, but this was a brazen act."

"What if the killer was in the back seat?" said Dave. "Waiting for Sabrina to get in the car?"

I nodded. "Maybe, but if he got in the car while the Friends-of-Ducks were inside eating breakfast, he'd have no idea when they were coming out. It could have been hours."

"I can't see it," said Nancy. "Say the killer is waiting in the car and Sabrina offers to give one of the others a ride home."

"Or someone happens to walk by," said Dave, "and sees him in the back seat."

"Too risky," I agreed. "It's too risky to wait in the car."

"A crime of opportunity then," said Nancy. "She had that rubber baby in the backseat with the umbilical cord attached. The killer climbed in and wrapped it around her neck."

"Or was invited in."

"Tell me again why we're looking for Bonnie Pickering," asked Dave. "Is she involved?"

"I have no idea," I said. "All I know is that she looked right in my eyes, denied being Bonnie Pickering in front of her duck people, and then one of them turns up dead. Plus, she was acting very strange."

"Yeah," said Dave, "but she knows that you know who she is."

"That's true. Still, it doesn't do us much good if we can't find her."

"Maybe she got spooked that you recognized her and killed Sabrina for some reason or other," said Nancy. "We can't rule out being mentally unbalanced. That's for sure."

"I hate to think I set these events in motion by calling her out," I said, "but you make a good point."

"So as I understand the situation," said Dave, "Sabrina Bodkin was killed either by one of the protestors that had a reason to want her dead, someone in one of her childbirth classes that had a reason to want her dead, or another random person that had a reason to want her dead."

"That about sums it up," I said.

"I'm going for donuts," said Dave.

Chapter 10

"The Extremely Reverend Biff Wellington is dead," Tryxee gasped halfway through one of our flights of fancy. "We need a new bishop."

I suddenly stopped in the middle of what I was doing, realization smacking me in the groin like that nun hitting me with a Book of Catechism.

"Hey, you don't have to stop," Tryxee said, but it was too late. I was already thinking about that nun.

"So why are you here?" I asked, hitching up my hauteur.

She flopped wantonly upon the wreckage of the davenport. "Isn't it obvious?" she churred. "We want you to be the new bishop."

I nodded adorably, yet clerically, and considered the opportunity. Sure, the perks were great. The big alabaster mansion on the hill, the luxurious silken robes, the fabulous dinner parties with celebrities, the nubile young handmaidens tending to my every want and need, and the special internet site of Bishop sermons written by unpaid seminarians. All that, and I'd never have to wear pants again.

* * *

I paid no attention to the choir as they ambled to their places for rehearsal, chiefly because I was practicing my postlude for Sunday, *Fiat Lux* by Théodore Dubois, a French Romantic composer. It starts quietly, and four and a half minutes later, the rafters are rocking, always a good thing on the last Sunday before Lent since there would be no more postludes until Easter morning.

"That piece is a bit meretricious for you, don't you think?" said Marjorie.

"Not at all," I said. "Where did you come up with that three-dollar word?"

"Word-of-the-day calendar," said Marjorie. "I've already used it five times today and I can't even remember exactly what it means. Something about whorish."

"Whorish?" said Lena from the alto section.

"Alluring by a show of flashy or vulgar attractions; superficially appealing," said Elaine, checking her phone for the definition.

"Well, it is that," said Meg, who had just come in with Mark Wells.

"I disagree," I said. "It's appealing, yes, but not superficially. You see ..."

"Blah, blah, blah," interrupted Marjorie. "What's the title?"

"*Fiat Lux*," I said. "Let there be light." I looked around. "We're still missing quite a few folks."

"They're on the way," said Meg. "The emergency vestry meeting is over, but Georgia is cleaning up a bit."

"Hey," called Bob from the back row. "Tiff and Bert are back!"

"We had to come back," said Bert from the back of the loft. "We heard there was another mystery story." He had his arm around Tiff as he ushered her to the alto section, then took his place beside Randy.

Randy shook his hand, then pointed to the chair on the other side and said, "This is Bullet." Bullet's hair had changed from yellow to white, I presume in deference to the last Sunday of Epiphany. He was busy poring over my newest apologue, but looked up, gave Bert a quick wave, and went back to reading as the stragglers made their way up the stairs.

"Bullet?" whispered Bert. Randy just shrugged.

* * *

"It pays three hundred grand a year into a numbered Swiss account," said Tryxee, straightening her lips which had gone strangely askew, "plus all your living expenses, and the continuing education allowance."

"How much is that allowance?" I asked, adding it all up on the Last Days Calculator I had stuck inside my copy of The Watchtower.

"Continuing education for bishops is open ended. Whatever you want, no limit."

I dreamed of the possibilities; travel to the holy sites — Rome, Constantinople, Dollywood, that Noah's Ark somewhere in Kentucky; Liturgical Lambada lessons; my own reality TV show.

"Why pick me?" I querreled.

"Because you're a bum, a rascal, a grafter, a blackguard, a profligate scoundrel." Tryxee suddenly sounded smarter, like that girl you ask to the high school prom because you think she's easy and kinda dumb, but then turns out to have won the science fair by dissecting a turtle in front of the judges ... a turtle named Shelton!

"Yeah?" I said.

"You know the lingo," she continued. "You can tell an aspergillum from a monstrance, a censor from a cincture. You can pass. And because once we get you into that Primate Peignoir, we'll own you. You'll do what we say."

"So that's the deal, eh? Sell my soul to become bishop?"

"Oh, they all sell their soul. It's just that you'll have a better deal. Don't forget," she coquetted, "I'm included in this bargain."

It was a bargain I didn't have to consider very long.

"Done," I said, "but let's get Biff Wellington out of here. I think his mushroom sauce has gone bad."

* * *

"I don't get it," said Bullet, shaking his head. "Can you just make up words? My English teacher would have a conniption."

"No, dear, you can't," said Rebecca Watts, the St. Germaine librarian.

"Of course you can," I said. "That's the way words are born. If Roald Dahl hadn't bothered to invent 'scrumdiddlyumptious,' it wouldn't have gotten into the dictionary."

"Is it?" asked Elaine.

"Yep," I said. "Now let's look at the anthem for Sunday, *Dazzling As the Sun.*"

"It's scrumdiddlyumptious," said Holly.

"At least we know what that means," said Bev.

Holly wasn't wrong: it is a scrumdiddlyumptious choral piece, finely crafted by Gwyneth Walker. Transfiguration Sunday in the Episcopal Church celebrates the event where Jesus goes up to the mountain top with James and John, is visited by Moses and Elijah, then is "transfigured" in blinding light, his face shining as the sun, his clothes white as the light. God then speaks from a bright cloud, "This is my beloved son, in whom I am well pleased. Listen to him." Transfiguration Sunday is celebrated on the last Sunday before Lent.

We went over the anthem that the choir had been rehearsing for several weeks. I thought it sounded good and we finished up with a flourish.

"The organ's too loud," said Bullet. "At the beginning."

"Huh?" I said, looking up, surprised.

"The first half of the piece must be kept subdued, except maybe where growth for expressing the text is notated. What about a different registration? Then, the climax in measure fifty-two will have dramatic effect."

I looked at measure fifty-two. He might have a point, but so what? The choir sat there, stunned, holding its collective breath. What to do? Destroy him now, or encourage his burgeoning musical intuition? My gut reaction was "destroy," but it was Lent, after all. Perhaps God sent me Bullet for a reason. I took a deep breath.

"You have a point, Bullet," I said. "I don't disagree. I thought you were a singer. Where did you learn the organ?"

"I'm taking lessons."

"Good for you. Let's try it that way and see how it sounds."

We did it again from the top. I didn't think it was much better, but maybe marginally better.

"Good registration," said Bullet, satisfied. "Just the ticket."

It hit me a second later ... registration ... ticket... I pulled out my cell and texted Nancy, then put it away. The choir waited expectantly. "We'll do it that way," I said. "And Bullet?"

"Yeah?"

"Never do that again."

* * *

When I got to the station the next morning, Nancy and Dave were already hard at work.

"I can't believe I didn't think of this," said Nancy, shaking her head and smiling as I put three big cups of to-go coffee on the desk.

"I forgot about it, too, till last night during choir practice. Luckily you still have those parking tickets, right?"

"They were right there in the trash can where I tossed them. Easy enough to trace the registrations."

Dave said, "Got 'em all," and looked up from his computer. Seeing the coffee, he hit the print button, then came over to the desk and took a cup.

"Bun in the Oven coffee," he said happily. "What, no breakfast?"

"Yes, breakfast," I said, and plopped a cardboard box onto the counter.

Dave opened the box, looked the collection of pastries over carefully, then chose a bear claw dripping with a sugar glaze still warm from the short trip across the street. "Five tickets, four names and addresses. I still couldn't find any more information on the murder car, but we're presuming that it was Sabrina Bodkin's since she was in the driver seat."

"Probably," I said.

"So here's the list," said Dave, pulling the sheet of paper out of the printer. "Bonnie Pickering's not on it, of course. She must have ridden with one of the others."

1996 Chevrolet Cavalier, Coogan Kilgore, age forty-two, single, actor, resident of Asheville.

2001 Ford Escort, Cyndibeth Lee, age thirty-eight, single, potter, resident of Asheville.

New Toyota Land Cruiser, Halbert Grayson, age fifty, divorced, systems architect, resident of Black Mountain.

2003 Subaru Outback, Ellie Darnell, age forty-two, single, title search professional, resident of St. Germaine.

I looked at the list: names, addresses, and phone numbers. With Bonnie Pickering, maybe the last four people to see Sabrina alive. Unless there was one more.

"Let's get in touch with them," I said. "Especially Mr. Grayson. That Land Cruiser's an aberration. The rest of those cars are junkers."

"On it," said Nancy.

* * *

Georgia Wester's worship and staff meeting had been hastily scheduled, but such was her ire that no one dared be absent. This was the largest group of attendees I'd ever seen at a worship meeting, Georgia having called in all the heads of committees. I wasn't even late, something that was known to happen with regularity. I had already taken my place at the table in the conference room. Marilyn occupied the seat to my left, legal pad at the ready. Meg was on my right, followed by Georgia and Mark Wells, the Junior Warden. On the opposite side sat Joyce Cooper, Caroline Rollins and Billy Hickson, all on the vestry, Marty Hatteberg, Bev Greene and Baylee Trimble. Jim Hook settled in the armchair at the end, looking haggard and worn. "I'd like to welcome all of you to the first worship meeting of the new year," began Jim. His voice was raspy and he spoke slowly.

"I'll take it," said Georgia. "We're in trouble."

Father Jim looked a bit startled.

"Say us a quick prayer," said Georgia. "I have another meeting in thirty minutes over at the bookstore." She clasped her hands in front of her and bowed her head perfunctorily.

"Oh ... uh ... well, let us pray."

We all bowed our heads and Georgia kicked me under the table.

"Heavenly Father, we come to you today asking for your guidance, wisdom, and support as we begin this meeting. Help us to engage in meaningful discussion; allow us to grow closer as a group and nurture the bonds of community. Fill us with your grace, Lord God, as we make decisions ..."

"A-hem," went Georgia, clearing her throat impatiently. She snuck a look over her folded hands at the priest.

"Umm ... yes ... as we make decisions, and continue to remind us that all that we do here today is for your greater glory. We ask these things in your name ..."

"Amen," said Georgia, then, "First off, we need to get Bev Greene installed as church administrator. It will be a part time position, twenty hours a week. We had a vestry meeting last night and everyone agrees. Bev has agreed as well." She looked over at Bev and got a nod in reply.

"I'll change the passwords, the signature cards at the bank, all the usual. Father Jim can concentrate on getting his health back. Marilyn will still keep the day-to-day calendar, and schedule the building.

Mark, you're in charge of the physical plant, everything else goes through Bev, then Father Jim for final approval."

I looked over at the rector. He seemed stunned by Georgia's speed and governance. This was clearly a man used to committees: committees that answer to other committees, then sit down and form a committee to think about a probable course of action in the near or not-so-near future, depending on recommendations.

"I ... uh ..." he said.

"This was what we decided last night," Georgia prompted. "At the vestry meeting."

Father Jim nodded and gave a cough.

"It's already decided and voted on," said Georgia. "No worries, though. We all know our jobs and it will make it that much easier for you."

"Oh." Pause. "Well, that's fine then."

"Now," said Georgia, "about these Lenten classes that have somehow sneaked their way into St. Barnabas."

"I'm afraid that's my fault," said Father Jim. "I apologize for my neglect."

"It's *our* fault," said Georgia. "We just didn't realize ... anyway, we'll take care of this from now on."

Father Jim said, "People have spent time and money in preparation. The classes may be a bit different from St. Barnabas' usual fare, but it may not be a bad thing. Our people may get a lot out of them."

"I agree," I said. "I don't think we can cancel anything at this point."

Georgia sighed. "Fine. Marilyn?"

Marilyn flipped to a different page in her pad. "This one meets on Wednesday evenings at seven. *Lose Forty Pounds the Yah-Way: God's Plan for Christian Weight Loss.*"

"I'm in," said Billy, and reached for the coffee pot sitting on the table.

"They'll meet upstairs in the Senior Ladies' Sunday School Room. It's being offered by Candy Waddle."

"She's a friend of mine," said Baylee brightly. "She's just an awesome Christian and she's done this program all over the tri-county area at different churches. It's a godly way to lose weight." She smiled at all of us, one at a time. "Really! Y'all come!"

"Perfect," said Billy, not returning her smile. "Sign me up. And pass me a couple of those crullers."

Marilyn continued. "Then there's the exercise class, *Paunches Pilates,* taught by Kimmy Jo Jameson. Tuesday and Thursday mornings at nine. They'll be in the parlor since it has carpet. Also, participants are supposed to bring a mat. If they don't have one, Kimmy Jo will have some for sale. There's also a fee for that one. Fifty dollars for the six weeks."

"That's very reasonable," said Meg.

"I think so, too," said Joyce. "A Pilates class over in Boone is twice that."

Marilyn continued. "If everyone wants to continue after Easter, Kimmy Jo says arrangements can be made." She turned a page. "Steve and Sheila DeMoss are hosting a new members and confirmation class for adults on Sunday mornings. Father Jim is teaching it."

"We'll have confirmation at the Easter Vigil if that suits everyone," said the priest. "I've already talked to the bishop and he's available."

It did suit everyone.

Marilyn said, "It's not a class, but Rodell Pigue and Sammianne Coleman still want to hold a meeting on the transgender bathroom policy."

"Why?" said Georgia.

"I don't know," said Marilyn. "Apparently, it's very important to them."

"Do we have a policy?" asked Caroline. "Is it even an issue?"

"I don't think it's an issue," Mark Wells said. "As far as St. Barnabas is concerned, all of our restrooms are single holers with locks on the doors. Anyone can use anything as long as they don't spit tobacco on the floor or try to flush a toddler."

We all looked at Father Jim. "I don't see a problem," he said.

"Okay then," said Georgia, "cross it off the list and tell Rodell and Sammianne we don't need a transgender bathroom policy."

"They're not going to like that," said Marilyn, making a note.

"What about the evil spirit thing?" asked Georgia.

"*Casting Out Unwanted Spirits: The Miracle of Essential Oils,*" said Marilyn. "This one is led by someone named Shenandoah."

"Goldi Fawn," I said. "Shenandoah's her new pseudonym."

"From the choir?" asked the priest.

"One and the same," said Caroline. "Goldi Fawn Birtwhistle. She's St. Germaine's Christian Astrologer."

"She works at Noylene's Beautifery," said Marty. "I have a coupon for a free reading and a haircut if you're interested, Father. Coloring is extra, though."

"*Christian astrologer?*" he said, flustered.

"Do we know what this class entails?" Bev asked.

"Yes," said Father Jim, "but I just forwarded this one to Marilyn. I didn't okay it."

Marilyn read from a sheet of paper in front of her. "Helping people reimagine themselves by using essential oils to banish unbidden destructive spirits."

"Huh," said Georgia.

"You know that's how our church burned down," said Billy. "Crazy people from the Episcopal seminary upstairs exorcising demons."

Father Jim was taken aback. "No, I didn't know," he said.

"I presume that Goldi Fawn will be selling these essential oils to her class," Bev said. "As well as her astrology and Life Coaching services."

"Lord, I hope not," said Father Jim.

"I think we can cross that one off," said Georgia. "You tell her, will you Marilyn?"

Marilyn nodded. "I'm afraid though, that Goldi Fawn has already planned to have a table at the Shrove Tuesday dinner."

"Okay, fine," said Georgia, her eye twitching just a bit. "But that's it. No classes."

"Any Lenten Bible studies?" Joyce asked. "You know, something that the church might actually have an interest in promoting?"

"There's a Bethany Moose Bible Study on Esther," Marilyn said. "Wednesday nights at seven, same time as the weight loss thing. They'll watch a video, then have a discussion. There are also workbooks and materials and such, available in the office. No cost to the participants, the church is picking up the tab. Luanna Mounce is in charge."

"Mom's going to that one," said Meg.

"Me, too," said Marty.

"Is that all?" asked Georgia.

"That's all I have," said Marilyn. "Except that Hayden has written a Lenten reflection for *The Bugle*."

"Wonderful!" said Father Jim.

I glanced around the table. Nine other pair of eyes looked at me in horror.

"More of a treatise," I said helpfully. "A comparative discourse."

"That's just great," said Georgia with a sigh. "Now let's talk about the rest of Lent."

* * *

Christy was at the counter of the post office, along with Angelique, even though there was no one waiting for any kind of postal service at the moment. That's the beauty of living in a small town: there's a lot of down time. The sorting had been done, mail boxes filled, paperwork recorded. It was ten-thirty in the morning. Christy was reading a paperback book, the cover portraying a well-muscled pirate, one hand wielding a cutlass, the other caressing the unabashed bosom of a comely wench. Angelique was sorting stamps, or at least I presumed she was, since there were stamps on the counter and she seemed to be moving them into piles.

The two women had worked at the post office for more than a few years, but weren't old — maybe early to mid-forties. They'd both been working when our post-mistress, Mary Miller, had retired. Mary hadn't been replaced and the two women handled the job with ease. Christy had dark hair, Angelique, blonde. They both wore the post office uniform.

"Morning, Christy," I said. "I've been looking for you."

"So I heard," said Christy. "I was off yesterday. I don't keep my cell turned on."

"Can you take a couple of minutes away from your book?"

"It is required reading by the Post Master General," said Christy, giving me a look. "*Imprisoned Passions*. There's a whole section on sorting zip codes while undoing your corset with just one hand."

I laughed. "May I borrow it when you're finished? I think Meg would like it."

"Sure." She put the book on the counter, pages down to mark her place. "Now, whatchu need?"

"It's about the woman who was killed."

"I didn't know her, but Angelique filled me in. Sabrina something."

"Sabrina Bodkin. Any chance you saw her car on Monday morning? It was a beat up blue Pinto. Might have seen her get in? Maybe someone else lurking around?"

"Nope, sorry. I don't remember the car." She looked over at Angelique. "We got here around eight-thirty and were here all day on Monday. Only a couple of people showed up that morning. It was real cold. There's not a great view out that window anyway." She pointed to the glass littered with taped-up announcements, lost cat flyers, and ads for buying ginseng, best prices guaranteed. "We did come out and look when the ambulance drove up. Besides," she added, "that window sort of fogs up in the cold."

"I can see that," I said. "Right now we're trying to find Bonnie Pickering. She was here that morning with the victim and all those protesters."

"The duck people. I saw those guys in front of the Slab. They squawked at me."

"Yep. She was with them."

"I don't know what to tell you," said Christy. "Bonnie was a friend for a while, but I haven't seen her for five or six years now. She worked up here as a sub, that's how I got to know her. We did some hiking, the three of us." She gestured at Angelique. "Then she quit the post office."

"You have no idea where she might be?"

"The last I knew she was living in Mars Hill but, like I said, that was a few years ago."

"Any reason you stopped being friends?"

Christy shrugged. "Lots of reasons, I guess. She was living an hour away and didn't come up here much. I didn't get down to Mars Hill and I don't chat on the phone as a rule. I certainly don't text. Anyway ..."

"Yeah," I said.

Chapter 11

The Slab was busy, even though the outside temperatures had not improved much. By the time Meg and I had driven down the mountain and into town, it was nine o'clock. Meg was taking the truck and going into Boone later, but had time for breakfast. Dave, Nancy, and Cynthia were already conducting the town's business around our official table, Cynthia being the mayor, Dave and Nancy comprising two-thirds of the constabulary force.

"Good morning, Hayden," Cynthia said. "And good morning to you, Meg. I'm just getting caught up on the murder case."

"Morning," Meg said cheerfully.

"Another couple of weeks?" Cynthia asked, glancing toward Meg's ever-burgeoning belly. "As your coach, I want to be ready."

"Hopefully that's all," said Meg. She took a deep breath then let it out slowly. "How *is* the murder case?"

"Not much closer to being solved," admitted Nancy, "although we did get in touch with all four of the duck lovers who drove their cars that morning."

"Not Hayden's old girl friend, though?"

"Nope," said Dave. "She's taken a bunk. She's in the breeze, off the griddle."

"All technical terms," said Nancy. "The Friends-of-Ducks are having a meeting on Sunday afternoon in Asheville though, and we're going to sneak down and infiltrate. Bonnie Pickering just might be there."

"My plan is for us to dress up like ducks," said Dave. "They'll never see us coming."

"It's good to have a plan," I said, dutifully pulling Meg's chair out since it was now obvious that she was waiting for someone to pull her chair out and Dave wasn't going to rise to the occasion. "What's for breakfast?"

"Pete's cooking up one of his famous breakfast casseroles," said Cynthia. "It has eggs, bread, sausage, cheese, basil, other stuff. I like it. Sticks to your ribs."

"Thanks, *dear*," Meg said, not unsarcastically, as she sat. I started to say something as I pondered for a moment that she didn't used to be so snarky, then closed my mouth and mentally chalked it up to fluctuating hormones, body morphing, water retention, and whatever else pregnancy might bring on.

Nancy obviously read my face and said, "It's not that at all. You're a pig."

"Yep," said Cynthia. "Pig."

"Sorry," I said for the fifth time that morning.

"Now," said Cynthia, "about this article in the *St. Barnabas Bugle*. It came in the mail."

"What article?" asked Meg.

"Someone, I won't say who, has written a Lenten Bible study entitled *Boxers verses Briefs, a Theological Perspective*."

"Oh, NO!" said Meg, her shoulders drooping.

"It's more of a comparative discourse," I said.

"Is your name on it?" asked Meg.

"Of course not."

Meg breathed a sigh of relief. "Thank heavens."

"I put *your* name on it," I said, a little sheepishly.

"*WHAT?!*" She turned to Cynthia. "Give me that paper!"

"But sweetie," I said. "You remember how you said you'd like to do an article for *The Bugle* but you just didn't have the energy?"

Meg growled. "An article on the coat collection drive for the Appalachian Mission Closet."

"Oh ... oops."

"Why don't I read it to you?" said Cynthia, a big smile on her face.

Meg's elbows rested on the table and her face dropped into her hands.

"*Boxers verses Briefs: A Theological Perspective*, by Megan Konig."

"Oh, Lord," moaned Meg.

"When attempting to understand the Ecclesiastical Underpants Disputation, we must finally ask ourselves — What would the disciples have worn under their robes, boxers or briefs?

This question itself contains the basic conflict apparent throughout New Testament Christianity: Grace versus the Law, Incarceration versus Freedom, Old Testament versus New, Subjugation versus Rebirth. Fortunately we can easily turn to the scriptures for guidance in these areas. When looking for enlightenment on underpants, we need go no further than Genesis 24.

Abraham said to the chief servant in his household, the one in charge of all that he had, "Put your hand under my loins. I want you to swear by the LORD, the God of heaven and the God of earth, that you will not get a wife for my son from the daughters of the Canaanites, among whom I am living.

He continues in verse 29.

So the servant put his hand under the loins of his master Abraham and swore an oath to him concerning this matter.

When studying this scripture, it becomes obvious that making a promise in Old Testament times was serious business. According to noted urologist Dr. Ken Dougherty, putting your hand under someone's loins and swearing is not a matter to be taken lightly. Certainly, Dr. Dougherty does it all the time, but he is a highly trained medical professional. Suffice it to say that the level of intimacy which this oath entails would not be possible if the oathee were wearing briefs. Therefore Abraham was clearly a boxer man.

We must also consider the passage found in Job. *Brief is the mirth of the wicked. The joy of the godless lasts but a moment.*

Can this scripture be taken blatantly out of context to make our point? Of course it can! As can many others.

Isaiah says it best in Chapter 33, verse 23. *Your rigging hangs loose: The mast is not held secure, the sail is not spread.*

Isaiah is an astringent personality, a prickly prophet, if you will. He is not happy with this move toward boxers. Consider his famous passage: *Surely he has worn our briefs.*

Here are the final findings of the Lenten Scripture Study on Apostolic Underpants.

- Adam - commando (pre-fall)
- Adam - fig leaf (post-fall)
- Abraham - boxers
- Noah - boxers
- Job - boxers
- King Solomon - boxers (silk)
- Isaiah - briefs
- Elijah - boxers (hair)
- John the Baptist - speedos
- Pharisees - briefs

- Sadducees - briefs
- Disciples - boxers
- Judas - briefs (extra-tight)
- Paul - briefs (pre-conversion)
- Paul - boxers (post-conversion)"

"Hayden!" cried Meg. "How could you?"

"Look at it this way," said Cynthia. "You are now the go-to expert in the field of Biblical drawers."

"You could get a book deal out of this," said Dave, "if you include some illustrations and a prayer or two. You should talk to Kimmy Jo. Remember? She made a fortune on *Victorious Secret: a Spiritual Guide to Purpose Driven Intimacy*."

"I think we'll all look back at this in a few weeks and laugh," I said hopefully.

"Relax, Meg," said Cynthia. "No one really thinks that you wrote it."

"Wrote what?" said Pete, appearing with four servings of steaming egg and sausage casserole.

"Apostolic underpants," said Nancy. "Who's wearing what and when."

"I heard about Meg's article." He put a plate in front of her. "Good for you, Meg."

"Arrgh!" she said through clenched teeth.

"More coffee, pumpkin?" I asked meekly. "Maybe a Danish?"

"We don't have any pastries this morning," said Pete.

"I'm happy to go and get you one, my pet," I said. "The bakery has some, I'm sure."

A low snarl was my answer.

"Well, I hope you're happy!" came a voice from the front of the restaurant. We all looked up as Goldi Fawn stomped across the checkered linoleum and huffed her way up to our table. "They say I can't do my class on casting out demons with essential oils."

"Yeah," I said slowly. "I heard about that."

"I do get to set up a table at the pancake dinner. They're letting me do that at least. Maybe I'll get some customers that way."

"I'm sorry it didn't work out," I said.

"It don't matter," she said, then pulled off her stocking cap and unwound a big woolen scarf from her neck. "I'm just gonna do it over at the Beautifery. It'll be another one of my ministries: Hair, beauty, reading the stars, and casting out demons with essential oils. Of course, I gotta have new cards printed up, and since I am, I'm dropping my professional name."

"Shenandoah?" I said.

"Yeah. It just didn't work for me. It's too confusing. I'm known as Goldi Fawn to all my fans."

"That makes sense," Cynthia agreed. "If I may ask, which oils do you use for doing your ... uh ... casting out?"

"Depends," said Goldi Fawn. "If you have a Demon of Flirt for example, I'll use a mixture of lavender, apple mint, and chamomile. If you've got a Demon of Shopping, I'm gonna set you up with some cinnamon leaf and organic sweet marjoram. That sweet marjoram also helps you through your flatulence. Cramps, too, so it's a three for one."

"This is amazing," said Cynthia. "I had no idea."

"I guess I'd better schedule an appointment," Meg said. "I have the Demon of Spousal Homicide."

"That'll be your Indian sandalwood and juniper berry," said Goldi Fawn. "It's also good for dandruff."

Chapter 12

"So tell me about this bishop," I said. "How exactly did you kill him?"

"Who said I did?" asked Tryxee.

I snorted. "It's obvious to a trained detective. From the clues, I can deduce that you and he were having a torrid yet passionless affair until, sometime last week, you found out that he was seeing yet another woman — brunette, beautiful yet mysterious, possibly Moldavian — and that she had her hooks into him like he was a catfish on the Feast of Carpus Crispy. He was passing her diocesan secrets and when you told the boss, Donald the Fig, he knew that your clandestine society, the Choralati, couldn't trust Biff any longer. So you brought him up to my office on the pretext of hiring me to snoop on the Unitarians, then you finished him off with poisoned lipstick. Judging from the smear on his collar, I would say Retro Matte Jungle Red No. 1."

"Ooo, you're good," she sniffed. "What gave me away?"

"It was the baby cows."

She shook her head in disgust. "Of course. The baby cows."

"And if you're a lyric, I'm Michelle Obama's anteater."

"Harrumph!"

We trundled the dead bishop out onto the fire escape and dropped him six stories into the dumpster. He hit like a bum being thrown in a dumpster: not a bishop, not a priest, not even subdeacon — just a bum, which just goes to show you that we are all alike when we finally take the Long Drop to Diaper Dell. The noise startled the occupants of the bin, a few rats, a couple of pigeons, and a guy we called Bassington, although he kept telling us his real name was Gerald.

"Hey," hollered Gerald. "Stop dropping bishops. This here is a nice neighborhood."

"Shut up, Bassington," I yelled back.

* * *

"We have some information," said Helen Pigeon. She had tracked me down and caught up just as Meg and I were about to make the trek up the mountain toward home.

"Helen, we're just on the way home," I said, knowing we weren't going anywhere soon.

"You should hear this," said Helen. "Meg, too. BLaM has detected some intel."

"Ooo," said Meg, undoing her seatbelt and opening her truck door. "What is it?"

"We should go over to the station," I said with a sigh. "Just in case this is something."

"Oh, it is!" said Helen excitedly.

The three of us crossed the street and entered the police station. Nancy was there, not doing much of anything, it being Friday afternoon. Criminals took Friday afternoons off — all law enforcement personnel knew this. Helen pulled out her big notebook, flipped a few pages and cleared her throat loudly.

"Okay," she started, "here's the thing. Sabrina Baldrick was a floozy."

"Bodkin," I said.

"She was a bodkin?" said Helen, looking confused.

"Her name," I said. "Sabrina Bodkin."

"Right," said Helen. "Sabrina Bodkin. She was a floozy."

"By floozy," said Meg, "do you mean that she had affairs with some of the married men in the birthing class?"

I looked at Meg like she had a squid sitting on top of her head. "*What?*"

"That's *exactly* what I mean," said Helen, amazement in her voice. "How did you know?"

"Yes," I said, "how *did* you know?"

Meg looked at me and sighed heavily. "Really? How did you *not* know?"

Helen said, "BLaM has discovered that Sabrina was playing around with at least one of those married men."

"How many couples were in the class?" I asked.

"Six," said Meg. "Two of us had coaches who weren't the fathers. Me and Cynthia, and a girl named Gina whose mother came with her."

"So four other couples?" Nancy asked, now taking notes.

"Yes," said Meg.

"She had a fling with at least one of the husbands," said Helen. "Could have been more, but we found out about one for sure."

I thought back to the one class I had attended, but couldn't come up with any of the participants' names. "I only remember four couples in the class," I said. "Us, that Gina girl, another big ol' boy and his wife, and that granola couple that wanted to birth their baby under water like a dolphin."

"Two came in later," said Meg softly. "Probably the second class." She looked uncomfortable.

"How did you find out about this?" Nancy asked Helen.

"BLaM is very active in the intelligence community," said Helen.

"Gossip," said Nancy, and made another note.

"Well," said Helen, "we do have our sources that we can't divulge. Certain people were observed and certain things were seen. Rest assured, our stoolies are fully certified."

"Iona Hoskins," I said. Iona had an old house just off the town square with a clear view of just about everything, especially from her rooftop balcony outfitted with a large reflector telescope.

"I'm not saying," said Helen.

"It's hearsay, Helen," said Nancy. "Nothing we can use."

"It's a clue!" argued Helen.

"Thanks for coming," I said, showing Helen the door and ushering her out.

"Wait!" she called, "don't you want to know ..."

The door closed behind her and I spun the lock. She gave a "harrumph" that we could hear through the glass, then banged her book closed and stomped off down the street.

Meg looked at me and there was sadness on her face. I nodded at her.

"What?" asked Nancy.

"One of those couples was from Valle Crucis," said Meg. "I can't remember their names, but Marilyn might have a record if she was the one that signed them up."

"And?"

"And the other couple," Meg said, "was Bert and Tiff."

* * *

"I guess I have to go talk to Bert," I said, once we'd gotten back into the truck.

"That just makes me sad," said Meg. "I'm sure Tiff doesn't know. Do you have to tell her?"

"We don't know if it's true."

"It's true," said Meg. "I guess I was trying to pretend that it wasn't, but I saw them ... Bert and Sabrina ... well ... coming out of the bathroom one night after class. No one else was around and I ducked back before they saw me."

"Why didn't you tell me this? I mean, right after Sabrina was killed?"

"I don't know," she said, and burst into tears.

Chapter 13

"I'm sorry I didn't tell you about Bert and that woman," said Meg. She'd gotten up earlier than I had and was already making coffee when I walked into the kitchen. Baxter was lying at her feet waiting for any kind of dropped pre-breakfast snack.

"That's okay," I said. "It would have come out eventually. If Iona Hoskins knew about it, everyone else will know about it quickly enough."

"I guess I didn't want to believe it. Poor Tiff."

"Remember, Tiff was the other woman less than a year ago."

"I remember. Do you think Bert killed Sabrina?"

"I don't think so," I said. "He is a suspect though. Would you like some scrambled eggs? I'm happy to fix them for you. Fresh, right out of the henhouse."

"Sure. Thanks." Meg eased her way to the kitchen table and collapsed into one of the wooden chairs. "Maybe Sabrina was blackmailing him."

"Maybe, but if Iona and you knew about the fling, you can bet that you two aren't the only ones. You can't blackmail someone if a bunch of people know the thing you're trying to keep quiet."

"Makes sense," said Meg. "So Bert didn't kill her. That's a relief."

"I didn't say that," I said. "There may be something else in play, something we don't know yet. I just don't think he did it."

I braved the cold and fetched a few eggs, then fixed my amazing scrambled eggs and cheese, French toast, and honey-baked ham breakfast. Amazing, because this was the first time I'd ever fixed it. Meg and I ate leisurely, enjoying both the coffee and the view out the kitchen window. We hadn't seen the owls since the cold had set in, but we weren't worried. I had made them a heated box out in the barn where they could get out of the weather. Barn owls were known to be less active most of the winter anyway — at least, that had been our experience with Archimedes. We always kept a supply of frozen mice outside where the owls could find them so hunting wouldn't be a problem.

A foot of snow was still on the ground and not likely to melt anytime soon. In fact, we were due for another dusting this afternoon. From the window, we could look out across the field to the river. There were three deer making their way along the bank and a good sized red-tailed hawk circling above them. Baxter saw them through the window and would have chased them off had he not been trying to make a piece of ham drop to the floor by way of some sort of canine telekinesis. Feeling sorry for him, I snuck a piece off my plate and under the table, only to notice that Meg was doing the same thing.

"I guess I'll go talk with Bert," I said as we finished up. "After I wash the dishes."

"The dishes?" said Meg. "You never wash the dishes."

"Well, you're pregnant. You should go put your feet up and relax."

"Wow," said Meg, smiling and struggling to get up. "Okay. I'm going into the living room and watching every episode of Downton Abbey. Drive carefully. I love you."

"I love you, too."

I was on the road twenty minutes later, heading toward town and listening to Thomas Tallis' *Lamentations of Jeremiah*. One of my Renaissance Lenten favorites, these settings of verses from the Book of Jeremiah are among Tallis's most expressive works. I drove slowly, thinking about death and rebirth as one does in the dead of winter, but mostly listening as the composer used all the compositional techniques available to him to squeeze every last ounce of poignancy from the text. Beautiful!

I knew the house where Bert, Tiff, and baby Charlene were living. It was one of the Pigeon's rental properties. I drove through town and took the highway past the Piggly Wiggly, Dr. Ken's Gun Emporium, past Tinkler's Knob, and finally turned on Laurel Avenue, aptly named as there were thickets of the plant flanking both sides of the narrow road. Bert's truck was in the drive, as was Tiff's little yellow VW. I parked in the drive and hiked through the snow up to the front door, looking the cars over as I walked past them. This was something that I had gotten into the habit of, over the years. A police thing: observe the cars. Bert opened the door before I had a chance to knock.

"Morning," he said, his eyes searching my face.

"I need to talk to you. It won't take long. Why don't you come out and we'll take a walk?"

"Let me get my jacket," Bert said. "I just got off the graveyard shift. Me and Wolfe Dickinson."

I could hear Charlene wailing inside and wondered, not for the first time, how I would cope with the same situation in just a matter of weeks.

"What's up?" asked Bert, pulling on his jacket as he closed the door behind him.

I motioned that we should walk down the road a bit and he led the way down the front path.

"Did you hear about your new job?" I asked.

"I did. I start in March."

"That's great. I'm glad it worked out for you."

"But that's not why you're here."

"No," I said. "I'm here about Sabrina Bodkin."

Bert's face fell and his shoulders slumped. "Oh, man."

"The word on the street is that you two were having an affair."

"The word on the street?" Bert said, horrified.

"Yeah. I think you were spotted. The grapevine in St. Germaine is not to be trifled with."

"Oh, jeeze. It was just a couple of times. Meaningless," then, "Who all knows?"

"I'm not sure who *all* knows, but Helen Pigeon knows. Iona Hoskins knows, I know, Meg knows, Nancy knows ..." I was counting on my fingers. "Cynthia Johnsson, Pete, Marilyn at the church ..."

"Jeeze," he said again.

"Look," I said, "I'm not telling you how to handle your own problems, but Tiff is going to find out soon. What I need to know is if you killed Sabrina."

He was taken aback. "What? Of course I didn't kill her."

"You might have, though," I said, "since she was blackmailing you."

"How did you know?" he said, then, "Oh, crap. I just fell for the oldest cop trick in the book."

"Yeah, well ..."

"Okay, she did try to blackmail me, but I don't have any money. I told her that."

"How much did she ask for?"

"Ten thousand at first. Then she said that we could work something out once I got the new job with that computer company."

"She knew about that?"

"Well," he said sheepishly, "I told her about it. Pillow talk, y'know? Then I didn't hear from her for a while. A couple of months actually. I thought it was over and she wasn't going to bother me anymore."

"It probably wasn't over."

"I guess not," said Bert.

"You were in the park that morning. You had breakfast with us, then went over to Eden Books to have your interview."

"Yeah."

"How long were you there?"

"I was there from nine-thirty till about eleven. Georgia can tell you. Then I went back to work around two."

"We didn't find Sabrina Bodkin until after lunch," I said. "Your alibi isn't that great, Bert, but for what it's worth, I'm fairly sure you didn't do it."

"Gee, thanks," he said.

"Sabrina was found in a beat-up '74 blue Ford Pinto. Is that what she usually drove?"

"No way." He shook his head. "She was pretty well-off. Drove a Caddy Escalade. Silver. It was last year's model I think."

"Look, we'll figure it out," I said. "If you didn't do this murder, there's nothing to worry about."

He nodded.

"But if you did, I'll bury you."

"I'd expect nothing less," said Bert with a forced smile and held out his hand. I was glad to take it.

* * *

Coming back into St. Germaine, my cell rang. Nancy.

"Are you in town?" she said.

"Heading that way now. I was just having a chat with Bert Coley. I'm pretty sure he didn't do it."

"Pretty sure?"

"Yeah. We're not crossing him off the list, though. Sabrina was about to turn the screws on the blackmail. As soon as his new tech job started."

"Well," said Nancy, "we found your girlfriend."

"Bonnie Pickering?"

"You have another girlfriend?"

"Listen," I said, "Meg's on the edge as it is. You gotta let this girlfriend thing go."

"Understood," said Nancy. "The point is moot anyway."

"How so?"

"Bonnie Pickering is dead."

* * *

By the time I got to the scene, the ambulance was already there. Bonnie Pickering was found by a passing motorist on Old Chambers Road. She was lying crumpled in a heap, off the shoulder, in front of a large boulder, her olive drab jacket speckled with snowflakes and almost invisible in the underbrush.

"A car hit her, or maybe a truck. She's been here for a while," said Nancy. "At least since last night. Her body is frozen solid."

"There's no reason for her to be walking out on this road at night. Too cold, too dark, too dangerous, too far from anywhere."

"You think someone brought her out here."

"I do."

"And she got hit by accident?"

"Or on purpose." I said. "What if whoever it was made her get out of the car and start walking, then came up behind her."

"She was hit about twenty feet up the road. One of her shoes is still up there and you can see some blood spatter. The impact knocked her all the way over here and she bounced off that boulder." The ambulance suddenly turned off its blaring siren. Nancy became quiet, and we listened to the sound of the wind for a long minute. Then she said, "The camera's in the car. I'll take some photos."

"Somewhere there is a vehicle with a heck of a dent in it," I said, "but I doubt we'll find it. Two duck people dead. What's the connection, other than the ducks?"

Chapter 14

We found Pedro LaFleur in the confessional at St. Mumford-Pancake. I knew he'd be there. Every Thursday he pulled down a few shekels sitting in for Father Graziplena who had a weekly appointment with his parole officer. Pedro was my goombah, my partner, a bad egg with a gun, an attitude, and more guts than a sperm whale, which holds the record for guts, its intestines being 984 feet long, exactly the length of the nave at St. Mumford's.

"Forgive me Padre, for I have sinned," said Tryxee, once she sat down on the sizzle seat.

"Not Padre," I said, squeezing in next to her. "Pedro."

"What?" said Tryxee.

"Pedro," I said. "Not Padre."

Tryxee gave me a look reserved for lunatics, ex-boyfriends, and presidential candidates. "Forgive me Pedro, for I have sinned," Tryxee started again.

"Save it, babe," said Pedro from behind the screen. "I don't wanna hear it."

"But my sins," she whimpered piteously yet wanly, "they're venial."

"I'll bet they are," snorked Pedro with a sharp, pinnipedial bark, taking the phrase "seal of the confessional" to its inevitable conclusion. "Stop blubbering. Now say two Hail Marys and balance a herring on the end of your nose."

* * *

Nancy and I rolled into the River Arts district of Asheville, an array of studios and working artists spread out along a stretch of the French Broad River, most of them housed in historical and old industrial buildings. Nancy had gotten the word that the Friends-of-Ducks would be meeting at Lavender Luna Pottery, the shop run by Cindibeth Lee. We left Dave at home even though he offered to come along dressed as a merganser.

We found the address then, after circling the block a few times, a parking place. The door was open and we walked in.

"We're not open," called a voice from a room in the back. "You'll have to come back another time."

"It's just us," Nancy called back. "The cops."

Four faces appeared at the door, all jockeying for a look. I recognized all four.

"How about some introductions?" I asked as they came out, one at a time.

"Do you have a warrant?" demanded the man I remembered as Coogan. He was still wearing the worn dark blue overcoat, something from the '90s with padded shoulders. He had salt and pepper hair, cut short, and a three day beard. He had a good-looking face and a cultivated expression of disdain.

"Calm down, Coogan," said the other man. I remembered him wearing a red scarf and hat, and a nondescript winter parka, but now he was in an expensive sweater and corduroys. He was fit and well groomed, sporting a pair of euro-style glasses: the odd man out in this crew. "I'm sure the officers just have a few questions. After all, one of our members has been murdered."

"Thanks," I said, as Coogan glowered.

"I'm Halbert Grayson," said the man. "This is Coogan Kilgore." He pointed at the large, florid woman from St. Germaine. "Ellie Darnell."

"I remember Ellie. We met last Monday morning during your demonstration."

"This is Cindibeth Lee and this is her pottery shop."

"Studio," corrected Cindibeth. "We do sell the pottery as well."

"Sorry," said Halbert. "Pottery studio."

"What's all this about Sabrina being murdered?" demanded Coogan, as if it was the first he'd heard about it.

"Well," I said. "I'll tell you. Sabrina Bodkin was found dead in her car a few hours after you all drove out of St. Germaine after having breakfast. There weren't many people out that morning as you may recall. It was bitterly cold. So you people are among the last to see her alive."

They stared at me.

"She was murdered?" said Cindibeth after a moment.

"Strangled in her car," said Nancy.

"My God!" Cindibeth dropped down into a nearby chair. She was wearing an old sweatshirt and jeans, and had obviously been working earlier in the day. She sported a ponytail and streaks of dried clay were evident on her clothes and in her hair.

"Certainly you don't suspect us?" said Coogan.

"Of course not," I said. "But I do have to ask you some questions."

"Fire away," said Halbert Grayson, pulling another chair away from the wall and sitting down.

Nancy pulled out her pad and began taking notes. "Coogan Kilgore, right?"

"Right," said Coogan.

"You have an occupation?"

"I'm an actor. I'm forty-two. I live at 67 Delwood Lane, Apartment 4A. My phone number is 828-555-2753. I have brown hair, blue eyes, I weigh one hundred eighty-two pounds, I am unmarried and gay. I like puppies, long walks on the beach at sunset, candlelit dinners, and honesty to the point of pain."

I had to laugh.

"Okay then," said Nancy, smiling in spite of herself. "How about you, Cindibeth?"

"Do I have to say how much I weigh?"

"It was sarcasm," said Coogan with a sigh, then, "I am surrounded by Philistines."

"Really," said Nancy, sounding equally as sarcastic.

"We just wanted to know what you do for a living," I said, "but I think we can figure that out now that we've seen your studio. We already have your other information."

"How?" Cindibeth asked.

"Because they are fascists," said Coogan.

"Your car registrations," I said. "We wrote you all tickets, although we tore them up later."

"Oh."

"How long have you had your studio?" asked Nancy.

"I've been here a year now."

"Any partners?"

"Well, we're in a committed relationship, but we haven't been married yet, if that's what you mean. Her name's Fatima. She's a performance artist."

"Any *business* partners," said Nancy.

"Oh. No."

"We know Ellie. How about you, Halbert?"

"Call me Hal. I'm a systems architect for Piedmont Health Care."

"You still live in Black Mountain, right?" asked Nancy.

"Same place I've lived for the past six years."

"What does a systems architect do?" I asked.

"I'm an IT guy."

I looked at him as if I expected more. He sighed, then obliged, giving what I presumed to be his pat answer to a frequently asked question.

"I create networking and computer systems. A systems architect is responsible for provisioning, configuring, and operating network systems. He offers technical support, and even research for long-term improvement plans."

"Sounds like a good job," I said. "Does it pay well?"

Hal glanced toward the other members of the duck group. "It pays well. That's why I can afford to help groups like this. I don't just give money, I also give of my time."

"You're a vegan, I presume," said Nancy.

"We're all vegans," sputtered Coogan. "What's that got to do with anything?"

"Nothing," said Nancy. "I just like to know."

"I am an Ethical Vegan," said Coogan. "Hal is a Biospiritual Plant-Based Vegan. Cindibeth is a Trans-Exclusionary Radical Feminine Raw Foodist, and Ellie is a Lacto-ovo Environmental Vegetarian."

Nancy didn't bother to write this information down. "How about Sabrina?"

They all looked at each other and shrugged.

"So," I said, "let's talk about last Monday. Did any of you see Sabrina get into her car?"

"I did," said Coogan. "I was parked two cars up from her. We all got in together and, I assumed, all drove away at the same time. I guess I was first in the line, so I didn't notice that she wasn't following."

"That's what I saw, too," said Cindibeth. "I was parked right behind her. I pulled out, but I waved to her as I passed and she waved back."

"I went out the other way," said Hal. "I was parked behind the library. I didn't see her get in the car."

"Me, neither," said Ellie. "I was parked beside Hal. He and I left at the same time."

Hal nodded. "I remember."

"Okay," I said, then asked, "When did you meet Sabrina? Has she always been part of your group?"

"Oh, no," said Ellie. "Sabrina joined just before Christmas. She came to our Winter Solstice celebration."

"December 21," I said. "Shortest day of the year."

"Actually, the 22nd this year," said Ellie. "We go out to the French Broad River Park and reclaim Santa Claus as a Pagan Godform."

"Really," said Nancy. This wasn't a question, and since I knew Nancy, I was sure she didn't want any further information on reclaiming Santa Claus as a Godform.

Ellie, however, didn't know Nancy and took the opportunity to do a little proselytizing. "Today's Santa is a folk figure with multicultural roots. He embodies characteristics of Saturn, Cronos, Father Time, the Holly King, Thor, Wotan ... " she paused. "I forget who else. Anyway, Santa's reindeer can be viewed as forms of Herne, the Celtic Horned God. We like to decorate our homes with Santa images that reflect his Pagan heritage."

"We stay out all night," said Cindibeth. "We talk and share the Great Mother's love. We sing songs to the Sun Child. At the heart of Saturnalia is the custom of family and friends feasting together. We all share about ourselves: our past selves, our future selves, our hopes, our dreams. That's what we do."

"Sabrina stayed out with you?" I asked.

"Sure she did," said Cindibeth. "She was a true believer."

"How about the other girl? Bonnie?" I asked. "Did she stay out with you as well?"

All four of the duck people flashed their eyes at each other involuntarily, trying not to move their heads. They couldn't have been more obvious if they'd been cast as extras in a 1929 silent film called "Who Killed Bonnie Pickering?"

"Bonnie Pickering," I said. "The one member of your group who doesn't seem to be here and that no one has bothered to mention yet."

"We don't know anyone named Bonnie Pickering," said Hal nervously. "The other girl you saw is called Bonnie Wentworth."

"We haven't heard from her all week," said Cindibeth. "I tried to call her, but it went straight to voicemail."

"You have a phone number for her?"

Cindibeth nodded and found Bonnie's number on her phone seconds later. She showed it to Nancy.

"Well, you won't be hearing from her anytime soon," said Nancy, copying the number. "She was murdered last night."

All four faces registered shock.

"Murdered?" Hal said.

"Now, tell me why none of you mentioned her," I said.

Four faces looked at each other warily, then Cindibeth spoke: "I called her after I saw in the paper that Sabrina was found murdered in her car. Of course, in the *Citizen-Times*, it was on page eight. I called everyone. She was the only one that didn't answer or return my call."

"We thought she might be in some kind of trouble with the police," said Hal. "That's why she said she didn't know you when we were at the restaurant. Maybe she was hiding out. We were just protecting her."

"How was she killed?" asked Ellie.

"Someone ran her down on the highway," I said.

"Probably an accident," said Coogan.

"We don't think so. Pretty coincidental, don't you think? Two of the Friends-of-Ducks members being killed inside a week?"

"Oh, my God!" said Cindibeth. "Do you think we're all in danger?"

"I don't think so." I looked over at Nancy.

"Nah," she said.

"You know," I said, "it turns out that Sabrina Bodkin wasn't the true believer you thought she was. She was a rather nasty person involved in at least one blackmail scheme that we know about."

More furtive looks all around.

"She wasn't blackmailing any of you, was she?"

"Certainly not," said Ellie, and the rest of the duck people agreed heartily.

"What I don't get," I said, "is why Sabrina came with you to St. Germaine to demonstrate. She was known in town as a birthing coach."

"She didn't want to, but Coogan insisted," said Cindibeth, pointing at him. "He said that we were all in this together and if anyone wasn't committed to the ducks, they were out of the group and should just go and join the Raccoon Society."

Coogan made a face.

"Bonnie didn't want to go either," said Hal. "We almost called it off."

Now everyone was looking at Coogan.

* * *

Nancy and I were getting back into my truck when we were stopped by Halbert Grayson's voice.

"Excuse me," he said. "May I have a word?"

"Sure," I said, and motioned Nancy into the truck while Hal and I walked off a few paces. "What's up?"

"You need to know that in the past two weeks someone has been accessing my private information and trying to run an identity theft scam on me."

"How do you know?" I asked.

"It's my business to know," he said. "Of course, I blocked it immediately, so no damage was done. They tried to open several credit cards, apply for a mortgage, access my retirement account, reroute my tax refund ... all kinds of things."

"Do you know who did it?"

"Of course I do. When I discovered all this I went right to the Federal Trade Commission. They don't bring criminal cases against identity thieves, but they do enter your complaint into the FTC's Identity Theft Data Clearinghouse, which the police can search as part of their criminal investigations. Then I went right to the police and, as usual, they did nothing. It's not their fault. They just don't have the wherewithal or the technology to do anything."

"Okay," I said. "Then ...?"

"Then, under the Fair Credit Reporting Act, I requested all information about fraudulent accounts and unauthorized transactions made in my name. I got that information last week."

"Who's name was on it?"

"No one I knew. It contained fraudulent names and addresses, but there was a phone number I recognized. I passed that information on to the police on Friday."

"Whose number was it?"

"Sabrina Bodkin."

"And how might that have happened?"

"Look," he said. "I'm divorced and Sabrina was a very attractive woman. She spent several days and nights at my house in Black Mountain during the holidays. I guess that she went through my files, papers, my computer ... whatever."

"You knew this before last Monday when she was murdered?"

"No, I found out a few days ago."

I pondered this information for a moment, then said, "Okay then. Thanks for telling us. I'll need her phone number."

"It's not her cell. It's a landline I think."

He searched his phone and held it up for me to copy.

"She was not a good person," he said. "She was using us."

Chapter 15

On Monday morning, I skipped out of the meeting at the Slab and drove down to Boone to talk with our friendly coroner. Kent was in his office when I arrived, puffing away on his ancient pipe, reading an edition of the *London Times*.

"What's going on in England?" I asked, flopping down in one of the two big leather wingbacks.

"How should I know?" said Kent. "This newspaper is from 1956. I like to read a newspaper now and then, but I hate what's in them. At least in 1956 things were more civilized. Nothing at all about Justin Bieber's latest love child."

"Perhaps, but perhaps the uncivilized was just under-reported."

"My point exactly. That's what we need more of. Under-reporting." He laid the paper aside. "How about a drink?"

"Sure," I said. "Bourbon?"

"I anticipate your every want," said Kent and pushed a full shot glass across the desk.

"Did you get a chance to look at the latest victim? I think her name is Bonnie Pickering, but she seems to have been going under an alias."

"Bonnie Pickering it is," confirmed Kent. "I checked with the Boone PD and they ran her prints. Her name popped up all over the place. She was a bad little girl."

"Really?" I took a sip from the glass, then looked at the bottle on the edge of Kent's desk. Jefferson's Very Small Batch Bourbon from Kentucky, the good stuff. I savored it for a long moment. "You know," I said, "I dated her for about a month back when I was a freshmen in college."

"I didn't know. I'm sorry. Here's her sheet."

He handed me a piece of paper and I looked down the list at the charges. Bank fraud, cellular phone fraud, credit card fraud, embezzlement, insurance fraud, welfare fraud, check kiting, and blackmail. Two convictions, one for embezzlement, one for insurance fraud. Fines, no jail time.

"Wow," I said. "I guess I'm glad we broke up."

Kent smiled. "Also, you should come in and look at her."

"Do I have to? She was pretty beat up. That car hit her hard."

"Yeah, she was and it did," agreed Kent. "Have another drink and come on in."

* * *

Bonnie's body was on the table and Kent had done his best rearranging her broken limbs into their normal positions. I could still see the breaks, the bruising and the contusions, but the blood was gone and, on the whole, it was much less gruesome than I expected. She was pale, of course, but I was ready for that. Her red hair had been rinsed out and dropped limply over her ears, pooling on the steel table. Red hair. I hadn't remembered that before, but now the memory came flooding back. Her face was well lined, yet it was a face I knew. She was thin, but did not look undernourished. Her eyes were mercifully closed.

"Vehicular homicide?" I asked.

"Most certainly," said Kent. "I think the car hit her going about forty miles an hour. That's about maximum speed on Old Chambers."

"You think it was a car?"

"Yes. Initial impact is high on the back of the legs, just about where a car's bumper would be, just below the buttocks. A truck would have hit her about a foot higher and broken her back on impact."

"You think she went over the car? Maybe bounced off the windshield?"

"Judging from where she was found and from the pictures that Nancy sent over, I would say not. It looks to me as if she went straight into that rock. Her neck's broken and that would have killed her almost instantly. Also, some ribs, both legs, one of her arms and a bunch of little bones. Both kidneys ruptured, spleen, liver."

"Yeah ..." I looked at the body and felt a sadness come over me.

"Here's the thing though," said Kent. "She had red hair and her blood type was AB-negative."

I thought for a moment. "Same as Sabrina Bodkin."

"Exactly. Now, natural redheads account for two percent of the population. AB-negative comprises less than one percent of all blood types. What is the chance that two unrelated women have both of these familial traits and are killed in the same week in the same little town in North Carolina?"

"Zero."

"Zero, or close to it. Sabrina had had quite a bit of surgery. Cheek implants, breast implants, a facelift I think, so you wouldn't notice the resemblance immediately."

"Sisters," I said.

Kent nodded. "I can almost guarantee it. Blood types run in families and so does red hair. I took a DNA sample from her and sent it in with Sabrina's, but I know what the outcome will be."

* * *

Meg had decided that it was time for a haircut: not for her, for me. I went over to Eden Books to see Georgia and look around for a new read. I found one by M.C. Beaton, an Agatha Raisin mystery. Meg had gotten hooked on these, and now I was reading them as well. Georgia had nothing pressing on the state of St. Barnabas Church so I headed next door to try out the new barber — Bill the Barber, as stated on the new sign above the antique red, white and blue striped pole inside the glass case. The pole was spinning and had a light on top. I walked in the front door and was greeted by 1955, come to visit.

There were two vintage red leather barber chairs in pristine condition, one of them occupied by an unmoving figure with a white towel wrapped in a circular swirl upon his face. Three smaller waiting chairs sat against the opposite wall. A stack of magazines rested on a small table. The counter in front of the barber's chair was long and white and had two sinks built in. The mirror, counter to ceiling, traveled the length of the wall. Barbering implements were arrayed neatly in glass containers filled with some sort of liquid that barbers know about. Clippers were in their places alongside towels, lotions, creams, handheld dryers, and an old fashioned radio. The floor had black and white linoleum tiles, exactly like the Slab Café. I wondered if Pete or Cynthia hadn't given Bill the Barber some advice on decor.

A man greeted me as I came through the door. He was dressed in a fancy white barbering jacket with pockets containing combs, little scissors, and who knew what else. His hair was slicked back and he had a wonderful little waxed mustache that would do Hercule Poirot proud.

"Good afternoon!" he said cheerfully. "Chief Konig, I presume."

"Indeed," I said. "I'm sorry I didn't come by earlier. I usually try to visit people when they come into town. You know, to say hello and welcome them."

"I appreciate that," he said, "but really, I've just been open since last Monday. I had scheduled my grand opening, but then that woman was killed right across the park. I thought it would be in bad taste. I didn't want any hard feelings right at the beginning. That's no way to run a business."

"Absolutely right," I said.

"So we've scheduled the grand opening for Wednesday. I hope you'll come by."

"Of course," I said with a smile. "Now, how about a haircut, Bill?"

"My pleasure, but my name's not Bill. It's Gary. Gary Tuttle." He ushered me into the chair and spun me around. "Gary the Barber has so little cachet."

"Oh. Okay, Gary. One haircut please."

"I don't give haircuts," he said softly, his hands caressing my head and face. "I offer the barbering experience."

The man in the other chair came to life. "Good afternoon, Hayden," he said, removing the towel.

"Codfish!" I said. "Good to see you again."

"You as well." Codfish Downs was a tenor, and a fine one. I used him on occasion when I needed a good soloist. Mostly, however, he made his living selling fish out of the trunk of his old Pontiac.

"I'm just here for a shave," said Codfish. "That and the ambiance. This shop reminds me of the one in my hometown when I was a little kid. Of course, back then, a haircut was thirty-five cents."

"And I could do it with a pair of dog clippers in a flat minute and have thirty seconds to spare," laughed Gary.

"How about some trout?" Codfish asked me. "I've got a couple of beauties left."

"Sure," I said and reached for my wallet. "Still ten bucks a piece?"

"Yep," said Codfish. "I'll get shaved and then leave them hanging on your truck mirror. They'll stay frozen for a month in this weather."

"Great. Thanks!"

Forty minutes later I was relaxed and revitalized. My hair had been trimmed by angels with silver scissors. My face was lathered with hot foam infused with apricots. I had been shaved with a straight razor, the long blade gleaming and capable of splitting a frog's hair down the middle. My face had been smothered with a towel so hot that it took off a few layers of unwanted skin. I had been splashed with Bay Rum, and it was delicious.

"Gary," I said, not wanting to get out of the chair, "that was a real pleasure. What's the damage?"

"For you, twelve bucks."

I got up and fished a twenty out of my pocket. "Keep the change," I said. "That was great. I'll be in next week."

The door to the shop opened and I felt the blast of cold air come in.

"Hiya, Chief!" said a familiar twelve-year-old voice.

I turned around. "Moosey! Nice to see you. Did you come for a haircut?"

Moosey had the most unruly hair in the town, maybe in the county. On a good day, it mostly laid down, except for the cowlick in the back that would not be tamed, not by scissors, not by gels, not even by glue (which his sister had tried more than once). On a bad day, he looked like a blonde hedgehog that had stuck its snout in an electrical outlet.

"Nah," said Moosey. "No haircut. Mr. Tuttle says I can come in for a piece of candy after school if I want."

"I've never known you to turn down a piece of candy," I said.

"Hey," said Gary softly to me, as Moosey went for the jar of peppermints on the counter by the register. "Watch this."

"Moosey, look here." He held out one hand with a dollar bill in it. In the other hand were two quarters. "Which hand do you want?"

Moosey smile up at him, crunched on his peppermint and took the two quarters. Then he ran out the door and disappeared down the street.

"I don't get it," said Gary with a laugh. "I try it every time he's in here to see if he's wised up. I guess they don't teach them anything in school any more."

"I guess they don't," I said. "Thanks for the barbering experience. It was great."

"Tell your friends," said Gary.

As I was walking by the Ginger Cat I saw Moosey up at the ice cream counter getting his favorite, a small fifty-cent chocolate cone. I opened the door and called to him.

"Hey Moosey, why did you take the quarters instead of the dollar bill?"

"Well, duh!" Moosey snorted. "Because the day I take the dollar, the game is over."

Chapter 16

I met Nancy and Dave at the Slab for our morning crime-solving confab. Another cold, cold day, another slim crowd eating breakfast out. Our mayor, Cynthia, was waiting tables as it was Noylene's day to open the Beautifery.

"Do you think we oughta take those wreaths down?" said Cynthia. "Christmas has been over for a month."

"Nah," said Dave. "I like them. They remind me of my Grandma's house. She used to keep the holiday decorations up until Easter morning."

"What's the word on the murders?" asked Cynthia. "As mayor, I like to keep abreast."

Dave almost made the obvious sexist comment, but Nancy slugged him in the arm before his mouth could open. I, of course, knew better than to say anything. That's what marriage will do for you.

"Don't say breast around Dave," said Nancy. "He's like a thirteen-year-old."

"I am not," said Dave, rubbing his arm. "I just possess a witty repartee."

Cynthia filled our coffee cups then took the fourth chair at the table, first wiping her hands on the dish towel she kept tucked in her apron. Cynthia Johnsson was possibly the only mayor in the state that was a certified belly dancer and it kept her in great shape. In my opinion, she was the second best looking woman in St. Germaine. She was also smart as a whip. Any double entendre by Cynthia was not an accident.

"It's not Dave's fault," I said. "Cynthia gave him the straight line. It's just polite to take it."

"It's true," said Cynthia. "Anyway, what's the scoop?"

"We were about to ruminate," I said. "Of course, it would be easier if we had something to munch on."

"Hey, Pete!" Cynthia yelled. "Gimme three orders of chicks on a raft, dough well done with cow to cover, and a full rack of Noah's baby."

"Sounds great," I said.

Pete's face appeared at the door of the kitchen. "I don't know what the heck that meant, but you're getting shrimp and grits."

Cynthia shrugged and said, "You heard him. Shrimp and grits. Now, spill it."

"We talked with the Friends-of-Ducks Sunday afternoon," said Nancy. "It seems as though Sabrina was running an identity scam on one of the members."

"I thought they were all Asheville crazies," said Cynthia. "They usually don't have much in the way of assets."

"True," I said, "but one of them is an IT guy — a big-time systems architect with a heath care firm — and he does have money. Sabrina spent some quality time with him right after Christmas and ended up with his Social Security number, bank account numbers, credit cards ... the works."

"He got taken?"

"No, he caught it before it happened. That's a perk of being an IT guy I suppose. Anyway, he found out who was behind it and contacted the authorities."

"She was arrested?"

"Nope. He'd just sent the info to the cops. Nothing had happened and he said that it probably wouldn't for quite a while. They are slow with these things. She was also blackmailing Bert Coley since she had an affair with him during the baby birthing class."

"Wow," said Cynthia. "Busy gal."

"According to Bert, it was a brief, meaningless fling, but he certainly didn't want Tiff finding out."

"Hmm," said Cynthia.

"It may be that she was blackmailing some other people as well, specifically, other husbands in the birthing classes. She seems to have found those classes to be quite lucrative."

"Really?"

"Really."

"Come to think of it," said Cynthia, "there wasn't any reason for her to be flouncing around in that midriff Lycra top and thong."

"*Thong?*" I said. "You guys never said anything about a thong!"

"Just that one time," Cynthia said, "and the men were sent out of the room for the demonstration. But, thinking back, she unquestionably made sure they got an eyeful before they left."

"What?"

"You don't understand," said Cynthia. "Everyone was talking about sex during late pregnancy, and uteruses, and cervixes, and just about every other part you can name. Photos and videos were being handed out, bosoms unveiled, enlarged nipples flaunted ..."

"*What?*"

"It's just a natural part of life," said Cynthia. "Meg and I talked about it, but it sort of seemed as if everyone was into it. We thought that Sabrina was a hippie and that the clothes thing was just to make it easier to demonstrate certain ... um ... techniques."

"*Techniques?*"

"Well," said Nancy, "she certainly worked that scam."

"The thing is," said Cynthia, "she wasn't a horrible teacher. She knew what she was talking about and everyone came away from the class feeling like they were ready for the birthing experience. Anything else that was discussed was just lagniappe."

"Smart girl," I said. "She took some classes, read some books, then bought the props and set up the classes. If that doula who was there for the first class I attended is an example of who's teaching these classes, Sabrina probably seemed like Madame Curie."

"I checked with Marilyn," said Dave," and she had the names of two of the couples that pre-registered. One was from here, Vern and Larry Jean Redfern. They live in a double-wide up by Ardine McCollough."

"Sabrina wouldn't have bothered with Larry Jean," I said. I knew Larry Jean. He worked a few cows, grew a plot of corn in the spring, and weighed about four hundred pounds. "No money there."

"The other couple was from Boone," said Dave. "He'd be worth a look. Jared and Linda Fish."

I laughed.

"What's funny?" asked Nancy.

"That was the couple intent on birthing the baby underwater."

"Huh," said Cynthia, smiling. "I never made that connection. Of course, I didn't know their last name was Fish."

"Jared Fish is a lawyer," said Dave. "I have his phone number and address."

"I'll talk to him this afternoon," I said, then turned to Cynthia. "Did Meg tell you she saw Bert and Sabrina together?"

"No, she didn't, but that explains some things. She was very quiet during the last couple of classes."

"Okay," I said. "It would be good to know about those other two couples. The ones that came in later." I kept looking at Cynthia, raising my eyebrows as encouragement to continue.

"I didn't know them and we all went by first names. Now I can't even remember those. It's been months." She thought for a moment. "Maybe ... Paula? No, that's not right."

"First names aren't going to help us much anyway," Nancy said. "Sabrina had the names, I guess."

"Do we have an address on her yet?" I asked.

"Nope," said Dave. "No known address. I'm sure she has bank accounts around, but they're not in her name, and we have no way of finding them."

"Here's something else," I said to Cynthia. "Bonnie Pickering, the murdered girl on the road, was Sabrina's sister."

Cynthia's mouth opened in surprise.

"Kent is almost positive," I said. "We'll wait for the DNA test to be sure."

"So now we have Sabrina and Bonnie both killed," Nancy said.

"They were colluding," said Cynthia. "They were in cahoots."

"Almost certainly," I said. "We checked the phone numbers that we got from the Friends-of-Ducks. Both their numbers went to a call center in Malaysia. They'd call in and get messages, then return the calls from an unidentified phone."

Nancy said, "Bert has no real alibi for Sabrina's murder, but he was on duty with Wolfe Dickinson when Bonnie was killed. I already checked on that. So he's in the clear for now."

"Well," said Cynthia. "Maybe Bert wasn't the only one being taken for a ride."

"Ha!" said Dave, but Nancy slugged him again.

The cowbell on the door of the Slab clanked noisily and the bevy of crime solvers that comprised BLaM came filing in.

"We thought you'd be here this morning," said Pammy. "We didn't want to miss the meeting."

"This is not your meeting," I said.

"Of course not," said Helen smugly. "We're just going to sit over here quietly and eat our breakfast."

They started moving a couple of tables together and were making quite a racket shuffling chairs and silverware. Cynthia got to her feet, picked up the coffee pot, and headed their way.

"Do we care?" asked Nancy under her breath. "We can always go over to the station and finish up."

"Here's our shrimp and grits," I said. "We'll talk later."

* * *

I called Meg when we'd finished. "You remember when you said that Sabrina was come-hithering the husbands?" I said.

"Yes," said Meg.

"Did you notice that before or after you saw her and Bert come out of the bathroom together?"

Meg thought for a moment, then said, "I guess it was after. Then, you know, it seemed sort of obvious."

"Yeah," I said. "Thanks. Have a great day. Love you."

"Love you, too."

* * *

Jared Fish was in court when I called and couldn't be disturbed. I left my number with instructions to return my call.

* * *

Fat Tuesday, the only liturgical holiday for the horizontally challenged. Our Fat Tuesday celebrations were relegated to the St. Barnabas Shrove Tuesday Pancake Supper, all you can eat for five bucks, all proceeds to the youth department. Shrove comes from the ancient word "shrive," meaning "absolve." This Tuesday before Lent is observed by many who make a special point of self-examination, of considering what wrongs they need to repent, and what amendments of life or areas of spiritual growth they especially need to ask God's help in dealing with. This is why we eat like pigs.

Seriously, Fat Tuesday (or *Mardi Gras* in the French), is the last big party until Easter. Once Lent makes its appearance the next day (Ash Wednesday), forty days of reflection and contemplation commence, at least during church services. No alleluias will be said or sung; the *Gloria* (Glory to God in the highest) is banished, replaced by the *Kyrie* (Lord, have mercy upon us); the organ postlude disappears; the Psalms become penitent. So, why not make the most of Fat Tuesday?

The parish hall had been festooned in the festive colors of Mardi Gras, purple, gold, and green: purple for justice; gold symbolizing power; green, the color of faith. Around the perimeter were tables, set up by enthusiastic purveyors of Lenten classes, all eager to have people sign up to better themselves in a strictly pious fashion. Goldi Fawn had quite a large display of her essential oils. I overheard her talking to Wynette Winslow and Mattie Lou Entriken, the matriarchs of St. Barnabas, apple-cheeked grandmothers, well into their seventies.

"I saw a woman in need and I just jumped right in," said Goldi Fawn. "She was sitting in my chair at the Beautifery, then suddenly, her head spun almost all the way around and she started cussin' me in unknown tongues. At first I thought it was because I left the yellow in her hair too long, y'know, and maybe the dye seeped into her brain. I use that *Daffodil Sundrop*, but it tends to burn the scalp if you don't watch it close. Anyway, then I realized she was having a Demon of Contrariness. I immediately tried a blend of pimento berry and carrot seed, but it just didn't work. Then it hit me: apple blossom! That did the trick."

"Well, I never heard of such a thing," said Mattie Lou.

"I suppose it could happen," said Wynette.

"Oh, you bet it happened," said Goldi Fawn. "And it could happen to you. It's a good thing I have all these samples with me today. Now, if you'll permit me to dab just a bit of this one behind your ears, I think you'll find that balsam fir is an excellent oil for calming muscles and joints after a long day or an intense workout ..."

"We don't work out much," said Mattie Lou.

"Other than trying to get to the bathroom," added Wynette.

I moved over to see what *Scripture Cookies Made Easy* was all about.

"Using this special tip on the pastry bag, I can get the whole book of Third John on one chocolate chip cookie," Susan Clark was explaining. "Yes, it's the shortest book in the Bible, but I think with a little practice, I can get all of Jude, all of Second John, and probably

Obadiah. Randy just loves Scripture Cookies. He eats them just like regular cookies."

"What translation are you using?" asked Monica Jones, obviously interested.

"You know," said Susan, "when I first started out I used the King James Version and the cookies were all dry and crumbly. But then I switched to the New International Version and they perked right up. Oh, yeah ... I also added chocolate chips, butter, and sugar, but I think it was the translation that really made the difference. We'll start out with just regular verses though, like John 3:16 and Romans 12:2, then move our way up to the harder stuff."

"I'd love to come. Do we have to bring our own supplies?"

"Nope," said Susan, signing Monica up for the class, "I'll bring everything we need."

At the next table, Kimmy Jo Jameson was dressed in her Pilates outfit, yoga leggings and a loose, off-the-shoulder t-shirt over a spandex top advertising *Paunches Pilates*. On the shirt was the title of Kimmy Jo's class, as well as a picture of a Roman prefect in a toga doing something strange with his legs. He did not look comfortable. Kimmy Jo was balancing on a large, bright purple exercise ball as she sat behind her table, looking extremely fit and ready to take all comers to the next level. Behind her, taped to the wall, were several posters touting the benefits of the Pilates method, as well as poses and exercises that would, no doubt, turn you into the person you longed to be. There was a line to sign up, mostly women, but enough men who thought Kimmy Jo might be worth watching for an hour twice a week.

On the other side of the hall was Baylee Trimble and her friend Candy Waddle. Their table was loaded with literature, books, videos and vitamin supplements. *Lose Forty Pounds the Yah-Way: God's Plan for Christian Weight Loss*. There were quite a number of folks in front of her table, and I supposed, like any other weight management scheme, that diet was the key, but prayer sure couldn't hurt.

The Bethany Moose Women's Bible Study had a table, and there were workbooks, reading materials, DVDs, paperback books by Bethany Moose filled with devotionals, that sort of thing, all provided by the church. Luanna Mounce was handing stuff out and signing women up. Susan Sievert was helping out.

As people finished perusing the church's Lenten offerings, they made their way to the tables and were greeted by stacks of Shrove Tuesday pancakes, maple syrup, sticks of butter, and powdered sugar. These pancakes, unlike other years, were a traditional pancake color, making them far more appetizing than in previous years where the cooks tried to create them in the greens and purples of Mardi Gras, but instead made them appear like badly digested cow-pies.

Along with the pancakes, being hustled to the tables by all the children of the church who could manage to carry plates, there was Community coffee straight from Louisiana, beignets from Bun in the Oven Bakery, and king cakes from Pat Strother, a local caterer extraordinaire. These cakes *did* have the plastic baby Jesus hidden inside, as Pat was quick to point out. "Bite carefully, don't break a tooth, and certainly don't swallow one," she said, at least twelve separate times over the microphone. Her warnings were heeded and we avoided a baby Jesus catastrophe once again. There were two babies to be found and the finders were crowned for the evening's festivities which included a game of *Is that Really in the Bible?*, a contest for making the best Mardi Gras masks, and, of course, a dramatic reading by Yours Truly.

The King and Queen of the evening were Ruby Farthing, Meg's mother, and Bud McCollough. Pauli Girl McCollough actually found the plastic baby, but she foisted it off on Bud once Ruby assumed the role of the queen. They were hailed, robed, and placed on a couple of fancy clergy chairs brought in from the sanctuary just for the occasion. The King and Queen awarded the various prizes and accepted their gift certificates worth twenty percent off purchases made in many of the downtown St. Germaine establishments, Blue-Rinse Thursday at the Beautifery not included.

Father Jim had begged off for the evening, still not doing well, and Billy Hixon was acting as the Master of Ceremonies. He introduced me as a pedestrian author, a mediocre talent, and a winner of several worthless awards in the field of horrible writing. After thunderous applause, I took the podium. The captive audience was enraptured, or at least, not too disgusted, and laughed when appropriate. I began at the beginning, reading the chapters the choir had already been privy to, then took the story to a whole new level — that level, according to Meg later, being "truly awful."

* * *

"You really want to be the bishop?" asked Pedro. We were back at Buxtehooters, sans the babe. I'd collected five sawbucks, my daily nut and retainer, and we were flush.

"Nah," I said.

"I'll do it," he said, twirling his moustaches like a Spaniard in a gender-neutral bathroom. "I'm tired of singing countertenor for chump change. Plus, I'm getting old, losing my high B."

"When's the Dittersdorf Competition?"

"This weekend," he said, "but I don't know if I'm entering."

"You're the defending gold medalist," I said.

"Yeah, but all these kids are doping. Steroids, EPO, HGC, blood transfusions ... they'll do anything to get that additional half-step, that extra appoggiatura. Sure, they have to pass the urine test before they sing, but if they're dirty, they show up with a clean sample in their Dasani water bottle."

"It's a different age," I said, sadly. "Remember that time you sang 'The Lost Chord?' Your cadenza went on for two minutes, the standing ovation went on for two more."

"Yeah," nodded Pedro, "that was a cadenza you could hang your washing on."

"It was a nine-point-nine-two," I said. "You got straight tens, except for that Russian judge."

Pedro smiled. "Anastasia Rasputin. I met her back at the Ritz, after the medal ceremony. She gave me a ten that time."

Ermentrüde came by with a couple of beers and plopped them on the table. "You bums got any geetus?"

"Sure we do, Erms," I said, stuffing one of my sawbucks down the front of her dirndl where it disappeared with a slurp. I pointed at the suds. "What is this stuff? It looks a bit skunky."

"The special. St. Bernardo's Dog Oil."

Pedro took a gulp, made a face, then downed the Dog Oil like he was running for bishop.

Which he was.

* * *

"Speaking of bathrooms," hollered a voice from the back of the room, "this would be a perfect time for our church to have the discussion of the transgender bathroom issue."

"Jiminy Christmas, Rodell!" said Billy. "Will you give it a rest?"

"We've been put off long enough," said Sammianne Coleman.

"This is not the time nor the place," said Bev. "We have kids running around here."

"According to the St. Barnabas charter," said Rodell Pigue waving a piece of paper, "any member in good standing can bring up a matter of concern at any formal meeting of the assembled congregation."

"Well, this is not a formal meeting," said Billy. "It's an informal party. So get lost."

"When is the next formal meeting then?" demanded Sammianne.

"How should I know?" said Billy. "Read your dang charter. That oughta tell you. Now, both of you sit down and be quiet while we listen to this real good piece of writin'."

We all watched as Rodell and Sammianne stomped out the back door of the parish hall. I watched them go, then continued.

* * *

I knew Pedro's plan 'cause I knew Pedro. He wasn't about to be owned by the Choralati. Once you're a bishop, you're a bishop for life. As far as we were concerned, the Choralati was just a bunch of entitled daisies in short capes, masks, and choir robes. They may dally in the bishopric flowerbeds now, but sooner or later, they would be dug up from the garden of privilege, and tossed on the compost heap of anachrony.

"Hey, you can really write," said Tryxee as we walked arm in arm down the sidewalk. "I like to be with a man of letters."

"It's true, Tryxee," I said. "I'm thinking about penning my memoirs."

"You'd better hurry up," she said, pointing to the window of the bookstore we were passing. Prominently displayed was a book with a cover that read "Autumn of the Shoofly" by C. W. Malooney, Jr.

"Why, that dirty rat!" I squealed, like a woman or some other squeally thing. "He stole my book title!"

"Pin your diapers on and show him the broderick, sweetie. You've been chiseled."

"Huh?" I said.

"It's eggs in the coffee. He pulled the grift, now he's gotta take the bounce."

"Yeah, yeah," I agreed, pulling out a pencil and taking notes. "He's gotta take the bounce." I was scribbling like a romance writer on Lady Viagra. Besides, in the long run, don't we all have to take the bounce?

* * *

"This is breathtaking," Marjorie said to Meg. "I'm on tenderhooks. I only wish I knew what the heck he was talking about."

"Tender what?" asked Meg, then, "Oh, never mind. We're all in the same boat. Some husbands go hunting, some make beer in the basement, some husbands enjoy woodworking ..."

Chapter 17

"If Sabrina and Bonnie were sisters, do you think they were running these hustles together?" asked Nancy.

"Let's assume they were," I said. "We don't know where either of them lived, but let's assume for the moment that they lived together as well."

"Would they have kept records on their marks?" asked Dave. He opened the box of donuts on the counter, chose a pink one with chocolate sprinkles and took a bite. Nancy and I were sitting in our official police chairs from Walmart.

"I bet they would have," I said, "if for no other reason than to keep the account numbers straight. In the case of Halbert Grayson, he said that Sabrina had gotten all kinds of information. She couldn't have kept all that in her head."

"So maybe on her phone?"

"We didn't find a phone," said Nancy.

"We didn't find a phone on Bonnie's body either," I said. "So maybe whoever killed them took their phones."

"Nope," said Nancy. "Well, maybe Sabrina's, but Bonnie was knocked into the next county by a car going forty miles per hour. It was dark, it was cold, she was well off the road. Nobody's going to get out and frisk her for a cell phone. Now, it might have been thrown clear of the wreck and is sitting in the woods somewhere ..."

"Maybe they didn't even have phones," Dave said.

"Maybe," I agreed, "but that would certainly be an anomaly in this day and age." Then, having an idea, I pulled out my own phone, found a number, and pushed the call button. A moment later, a voice answered on the other end. I put the phone on speaker.

"Hi, Bert. This is Hayden."

"Yeah, Hayden. What do you need?"

"Sabrina Bodkin. Did she have a cell phone?"

"Not that I knew about. She gave me a story about how cell phones cause brain tumors, that her brother died of one, and that she wasn't about to be next. I don't know if I believed her or not, but I never saw her with one."

"Is that an actual thing? Brain tumors?"

"Well, I looked it up and it seems like it is. The data doesn't seem to support the claim but, if you ask me, it's one of those things that no one is sure about."

"How did you get in touch with her then? Did you have to leave a message with her service?"

"Nope," said Bert. "She had a phone I guess, but I never called her. I didn't even have the number. She'd call me. The caller ID would always pop up 'unknown number' and that would be her."

"You didn't find that a bit odd? The woman with whom you're having an affair didn't give you a number where you could reach her?"

I could hear Bert sigh over the phone. "It was just a couple of times," he said. "After that, she was blackmailing me and I didn't really want to call her, y'know?"

"Okay," I said. "Thanks. And Bert?"

"Yeah?"

"Don't leave town."

"Very funny," he said, and hung up.

"No cell phone," said Nancy. "What do you bet that Bonnie had the same phobia?"

"Interesting," I said.

The door to the station opened and Helen Pigeon walked in. "We need to search the murder car," she announced.

"The murder car," said Nancy.

"Yes, the Ford Pinto. We think there are clues."

"Helen," said Nancy, "there are no clues, and even if there were, you can't search it. It's in the police lot over in Boone."

"Can't you write us a note?" asked Helen. "Please? We've hit a dead end."

"Helen," I said. "Why don't you get BLaM to investigate that missing cat over on Oak Street, the one that's on all the flyers around town. You're a crime club aren't you?"

"Blueridge Ladies of *Murder*," said Helen. "Murder, not stupid lost cats!" She turned on her heel and stormed out.

We watched her through the plate glass as she crossed the street and headed across the park.

"Sabrina might have the information at her house, wherever that is," said Dave, now on his second donut.

"Or in her car," I said. "Bert told me that she usually drove a Cadillac Escalade. My thought is that she would have kept them with her, even in that piece of trash Pinto."

"We searched it," said Nancy. "Nothing."

"What did we pull out?" I said. "Books, an old guitar, and the baby doll?"

"A blanket," said Dave, "and a grocery bag."

"Why would you have a guitar with no strings in the back seat?" I asked. "Where is that thing?"

"I'll get it," said Nancy, and she disappeared into the back room for a moment, then reappeared with the guitar in hand. It was an old junker, classical style with a Yamaha sticker on the headstock. She handed it to me and I peered inside. Nothing that I could see.

"Reach in there," I said to Nancy, "and see if you feel anything. My hands are too big."

She did and shook her head, then crooked her hand a bit more and her face lit up.

"Ha!" She pulled her hand out and in it was an envelope with a piece of duct tape across the width of it, two ends sticking out where the tape had been holding the envelope in place.

"What do you know?" she said, and opened the envelope. "Police work triumphs again. I'm just glad Helen Pigeon wasn't here to see this." She spread the papers out on the counter in front of us.

Gibberish, five pages worth, all printed from a computer using a laser printer.

```
w2=36CE vC2JD@? d_[ _c`d`hea $$Rbdc\gec\__ab
#@FE:?8 }@] ceaghfebc p44E }@] ghecdab``a !9]
gagcbfhgcd |2DE6Cr2C5 agfegdbcadeh__gf 6IA _ha_`h
p>tlagefcdb`cefdgh_d 6IA _ca_`e {:?6 @7 4C65:E q2?<
@7 p>6C]aacbhefade 'x$pg___hefcbegefc`a6IA`aa_`f
w@>66BF:EJ agf_hdech_
```

"It's all encoded," said Dave. "That figures."

"I've never seen anything like that," I said.

"Nor I," agreed Nancy.

"We obviously need someone who knows about this stuff," I said.

"How about Bert?" asked Nancy.

"He's too close to it," I said. "I can take it up to the computer department at Appalachian State. I know a guy."

* * *

The guy I knew was Dr. Neeraj Agrawal, head of the computer science department. I'd met him a few months before at a library function that Meg had dragged me to. I called his secretary and managed an appointment just before lunch.

Dr. Agrawal was in his late twenties, and the word was that he was on his way up in academia, or, if he chose, into the super-rich world of the computer elite, or both. He had been one of those child geniuses who grew up into an adult genius. I was ushered into his office and found him with his feet up on his desk, eyes closed, fingers interlaced behind his head. He had Indian features and coloring and he wore a pair of wire rimmed glasses, jeans, worn cowboy boots, and a black t-shirt advertising a band called *The Carburetors*. I'd heard that band, I thought. He opened his eyes.

"Detective Konig," he said when he saw me. "Please have a seat and tell me what I can do for St. Germaine's finest."

"I'm surprised you remember me," I said.

"The blessing of an eidetic memory. How's Meg? That baby is just about due, isn't she?"

"She's almost here, thanks."

"Little Abigail, right?" He knew perfectly well he was right.

"That's the current name on the list, but we'll have to see if it suits her after we meet her."

"Very wise," he said. "My father and my uncles wanted to name me Avinash, which is a family name, but my mother thought I looked more like a Neeraj. How right she was."

"I can not help but agree," I said.

"How may I be of service? I have a meeting in about four minutes."

I spread the pages out in front of him and he looked at them for a full two of the allotted four minutes.

"Am I to presume this has something to do with the two murder cases you have in St. Germaine at the moment? I read about them in the paper."

"Yes. The two victims were running scams and blackmail schemes on a number of people. This is probably a record of the people they were targeting. Maybe the killer is on that list somewhere."

"Ah." He adjusted his glasses. "Then I won't charge you my usual two thousand an hour."

"Thanks," I said, nervously.

"I'm just kidding," he replied, laughing. "This is a cipher that uses an alphabet that is a subset of ASCII characters."

"The characters used by computer language?"

"Yes," he said. "ASCII — American Standard Code for Information Interchange — is the character encoding standard, although it goes by different names now. ASCII codes represent text in computers, telecommunications equipment, devices like that. There are ninety-four printable characters, and this seems to be a simple cipher that replaces one character with another. All the characters are available to you on your standard keyboard. The trick is to find which characters are replaced by which."

"Sounds like a long process," I said.

"It's not so bad," he said. "The chances are good that this cipher simply shifts the character set to a new position. For example, what we call a ROT13 cipher would replace any character with the one located thirteen positions after it in the ASCII alphabet. Since there are ninety-four characters, a random replacement scheme would really be too cumbersome to decipher quickly and probably wouldn't be used, not by your criminals. You see, here is the crux of the argument. Someone who is really good wouldn't use this cipher — they'd use something much more sophisticated — and someone who isn't so good wouldn't use a random replacement scheme. Follow?"

"I think so."

"Even if they did, there are only eight thousand, eight hundred thirty-six possible two letter substitution combinations. If I'm right though, it should be a simple matter of discovering what key was used. After that, easy."

"How long will that take me?"

"You? A few weeks perhaps, if you work on it full time." He looked at the papers in front of him again. "Do you have any name you can give me, or something that you're sure would appear in the text once it was deciphered?"

"Halbert Grayson," I said.

"I can write a quick program when I get back from my lunch meeting. I should have something for you this afternoon. While I'm at lunch I'll have one of my grad assistants type these pages into a document we can use."

"Thanks! I'm just curious. How long will it take you to write such a program?"

"Three minutes, thirteen seconds."

I stood and shook his hand. "Thank you, Dr. Agrawal."

He gave me a big smile. "Call me Neeraj."

* * *

Dave called me on the way back to St. Germaine. "I checked on Bonnie's and Sabrina's brother in Cary. Quinn Pickering. We were right, by the way. They were sisters. Quinn died five years ago of a malignant brain tumor. The parents are involved in some class action suit against AT&T."

Chapter 18

We found C. W. Malooney, Jr. sitting at a table in the Books-a-Million, autographing copies hand over fist.

"You want an autograph?" he smirked greasily. "You gotta buy a book if you want an autograph. It'll cost you $26.95."

"Not a chance," I gristled.

"You should get one," said Tryxee, skimming the contents. "It looks pretty good."

"Yeah?"

"Yeah. Listen to this: The Case of the Missing Mohair, The Case of the Crinkled Crinolines, the Case of the Limping Leprechaun, The Case of the Vapid Vampire ... "

"All my cases!" I shouted. "You not only stole my title, you stole my cases!"

"Just bar stories," said C. W. Malooney, Jr. with a shrug. "Could have been anyone's really. Might have been mine for all I can remember."

"Fog him, Sweetums," said Tryxee. "Give him the bump off."

I pulled out my Chicago typewriter and let him have it right between graphic novels and literary criticism: wubba barked the gat, wubba, wubba, wubba.

Tryxee's eyes went wide. "Wow, you really did it. He was gonna be on 'Ellen' tomorrow. Now he's cold ham and Swiss. He's got more holes in him than one of your plots."

"Nice simile," I said, admiring the twin spires of her intellect for the third time in the last five minutes. "Besides, I never liked Malooney," I said. "He was a dirty plagiarist. Those stories are mine."

"Plagiarism is a horrible, horrible thing," said Tryxee, her eyes filling with tears.

* * *

"Here are two questions we have not yet considered," I said. "Why was Sabrina driving the Pinto when she had a Cadillac, and why was she just sitting in her car with the engine running as someone snuck up behind her and did her in?"

Meg, Cynthia, and Pete were all sitting at the table with me at the Bear and Brew, Pete leaving the Slab under the watchful eye of Noylene and Manuel Zumaya, the Slab's short order chef.

"Isn't today a day for fasting?" asked Cynthia. "Ash Wednesday, I mean. You should be fasting and repenting."

"I should," I said, "but I'm not. I'm having the large Black Bear pizza and an Absolom's Ale. I've had a hard week. Who's in?"

"I'm in on that pizza," said Pete. "I'll have to peruse the beer list."

"I've decided to go through it alphabetically," I said. "One beer at a time. There are forty on the list. That's my Lenten discipline."

"*Really?*" said Meg, sounding appalled. "That's your Lenten discipline? Shouldn't you be contemplating your own mortality or something?"

"That's why I'm starting with a pale ale," I said.

"That's a fine Lenten discipline," said Pete. "To show my solidarity, I shall join you in your pietistical reflection."

"The pizza's fine with me," said Cynthia. "No beer, just water."

"I'd just like a salad," said Meg, "and a glass of water. If I get any bigger, I'll get stuck in the bathtub and the paramedics will have to harpoon me to get me out."

Our waitress, a smallish waif named Ginny, according to her name tag, took our order and disappeared.

"Hey, you guys," said a voice behind me.

"Hi, Angelique," said Meg, looking over my shoulder. I turned around in my chair and smiled a greeting. Angelique was in her post office parka, something left over from the days where she delivered mail.

"I suggest the Black Bear pizza," I said.

"We're having sandwiches," said Angelique. "I'm just picking them up. Christy's minding the store."

Cynthia said, "Hayden told us that you knew Bonnie Pickering."

Angelique's face clouded and she shook her head sadly. "Christy knew her better than I did, but she worked at the post office as a sub. I liked her. She was a sweet girl."

"I'm sorry," Cynthia said.

"Before she disappeared, you know, about five years ago, sometimes the three of us would do stuff together on Monday holidays. Hiking mostly. Mount Mitchell, Grandfather Mountain, Chimney Rock ... things like that."

"We should do that," Meg said to me. "You never take me hiking."

"You're nine months pregnant," I said, then corrected myself immediately. "Not that that's any kind of impediment."

"After the baby's born," said Meg. "I mean, *really!*"

"I like to hike Grandfather," said Cynthia.

"Me, too," said Pete.

"You've never hiked in your life!" said Cynthia. "Well, maybe to the refrigerator for a beer."

"I've hiked Grandfather Mountain," I said. "I believe it was in 1979."

"I love that hike," said Angelique, smiling. "You know, until all this happened, I hadn't thought about Mildred the Bear in ages and ages."

"There's a trail that goes up to Linville Falls that's really fun," said Cynthia. "You and Christy should try that one."

"I think we'll wait until spring," said Angelique. "I have no desire to hike when it's twenty degrees outside."

"Here's your order," said Ginny, walking up with a white paper bag in her hand. "Two meatball subs."

"Thanks," said Angelique, and took the bag. "I'll see you later," she said. Then she gave a small wave and headed for the door.

"Now, what's all this about a Cadillac?" asked Cynthia, once Angelique had gone.

"According to Bert Coley, and others around town, specifically those who saw her drive in for birthing classes, Sabrina Bodkin drove a silver Cadillac Escalade."

"I never saw what she drove," said Meg. "I guess she parked in the back somewhere."

"Me, either," said Cynthia. "That's an expensive car, though."

"It was last year's model. Sabrina was doing very well for herself."

"She probably drove that Pinto because she was trying to blend in with the duck people," said Pete. "Most of those guys are not driving Caddies."

"Halbert Grayson had a late model Land Cruiser," I said. "That's not cheap, but I think you're right."

"She was going incognito," said Cynthia. "No makeup, stocking cap, coveralls. She didn't want to be recognized. She would have been spotted in that Escalade."

"But why?" asked Meg. "Why come into town at all?"

"Coogan Kilgore told the Friends-of-Ducks that they were all expected to be there. He was adamant, in fact."

"Who is Coogan Kilgore?" asked Meg.

"He's their leader, I guess," I replied. "Unofficially, anyway. That's the only reason that Bonnie Pickering came along as well. My guess is that they were playing the marks, Halbert specifically, and needed to be part of the group, at least for a while longer."

Our two beers (and two waters) were delivered, set down in front of us, and Pete and I embarked upon our forty beer pilgrimage.

"So, no one would have recognized Sabrina driving her unregistered Ford Pinto, and wearing insulated coveralls," said Cynthia.

"Someone recognized her," I said.

"What about Tiff?" said Pete. "Jealousy is a powerful motive for murder. Did you think about her?"

"About a hundred times," I said. "She's definitely a suspect, although we haven't talked to her yet."

"Bert was on duty the night that Bonnie was killed, right?" said Meg.

"Right."

"Tiff stays with her mom on the nights that Bert works. She told me that when we were chatting during choir rehearsal."

"That's a good thing to know," I said. "I'll check on that. I looked at her VW when I was at their house. Bert's truck, too. No damage to either one."

"That doesn't mean anything, does it?" asked Cynthia. "Either one of them could have gotten a different car."

"True, but if Tiff was at her mom's house, they're both alibied up."

Cynthia said, "Someone would had to have known Sabrina really well to recognize her."

"Yep," I said. "On to the second question. Why was she just sitting in her car? Kent said that there were no indications that she struggled at all when the umbilical cord was tied around her neck. It was pulled tight, tied, and the stretchy latex did its work."

"She was knocked out," said Pete. "That's the only explanation. I like this beer, by the way. Refreshing!"

"So," said Meg, "maybe one of the Friends-of-Ducks put something in her breakfast while they were eating over at the Slab that morning. Something that would knock her out."

"Kent Murphee checked for that," I said. "He did all the normal blood work. Nothing of the kind showed up."

"What about something in the car?" asked Cynthia. "A faulty exhaust for instance."

"We checked the car. The exhaust system wasn't great, there were holes in the muffler and the main pipe, but the car was sitting outside. It wasn't in any kind of sealed environment."

"Huh," said Meg. "Well, I don't know then."

Our lunch showed up at the table, an extra-large Black Bear Attack Pizza, the specialty of the house: homemade bear sausage, Black Krim heirloom tomatoes, truffles, mushrooms, and a double helping of mozzarella cheese. Also appearing was Meg's salad: a small bowl of arugula, broccoli, and bean sprouts, drizzled with a soupçon of olive oil.

"Gimme a piece of that pizza," Meg growled, "and a beer."

"Meg, think of little Albuquerque, or whatever her name is," said Pete, grinning.

"Grrrr."

"Here," I said, pushing my glass across the table, "have mine. I'm sure that Abigail will understand." I waved our waitress over and ordered another, this time Brettaberry Farmhouse Ale, next on the alphabetical list.

"If I eat another salad, I will absolutely go comatose!"

"Comatose," I repeated, then sat still for a long moment.

Meg looked at me, then said, "You have an idea, don't you?"

"Hmm," I said. "I'll bet I know the reason that Sabrina passed out."

"Why?" asked Cynthia, already digging into her slice.

Pete and Meg looked at me, expectation on their faces.

"Something she ate."

"What?" said Pete, raising both hands. "I fixed everybody pancakes. We all ate them."

"*Gluten-free* pancakes," I said.

"No, they weren't," said Pete. "I don't have any gluten-free pancakes."

"Exactly."

* * *

Jared Fish called me back at two in the afternoon. Our conversation was short and sweet, the gist of it going like this:

Me: Pleasantries, then, "Did you have an affair with Sabrina Bodkin, your birthing coach, after which she was blackmailing you?"

Mr. Fish: "You'll be hearing from my lawyer."

Click.

An admission if ever I heard one.

Chapter 19

"How are you gonna tie all this together?" asked Pedro. "You've got too many story lines going."

It was true. I'd written myself into a corner like that Little Jack Horner guy scribbling pie recipes. Still, I'd been in worse literary fixes and besides, I always had Deus Ex Machina to fall back on.

"I dunno," I said.

"You've got Bishop Biff Wellington, you've got baby cows ..."

I nodded.

"You've got Tryxee Gale, the Choralati, and now you've put C. W. down for a dirt nap."

"He had it coming."

"I never said he didn't," said Pedro, taking a puff on his stogy. "Nobody liked him anyway." He gave me the look, then said, "Don't even think about Deus Ex Machina. You use that one more time and you're outta the writing game."

I considered the possibility.

He was counting on his fingers now: "You've got Ermentrüde, Bassington, a beautiful yet mysterious Moldavian woman, St. Mumford-Pancake, and the Dittersdorf competition. You've got me running for bishop. You've still got Stink-Eye Lewis and Jimmy Snap, not to mention Rex the famous detecting dog."

"Anybody else?" I sighed.

"Yeah. The Big Schlemiel and Donald the Fig."

"The key here," I said foxily, is to get everyone in the same room, come up with a clever plot, then tie it all together, solve the case in one fell swoop, collect our cash, and go have a drink."

"It's a plan," said Pedro. "You want I should call the coppers?"

"Yeah," I agreed. "We oughta have coppers."

* * *

Nancy and I drove up to Bert and Tiff's house. Bert's truck was gone, it being the middle of the afternoon and Deputy Coley still working for the sheriff's department. The house was a single story Craftsman style cottage, left over from the days when the good and great had summer places up here in the mountains to escape the heat of the lowlands. It was a white clapboard with moss-green shutters and had probably been updated over the years with insulation, heat and air, and electrical wiring that was several steps beyond the old knob and tube stuff that was prevalent in the 1920s when it was built. I say *probably* because there were still a number of old cottages in our area that had never been renovated. I didn't see Bert and Tiff and a new baby living in one of those, however. What I knew of Tiff led me to expect her living quarters to be well appointed. Also, Jeff and Helen Pigeon were not slumlords. Their properties tended to be rather upscale and command top prices in the rental market: hardwoods, shaker-style kitchens, subway tiles, granite, stainless, natural light, open concept ... all the buzzwords that made a house a home for a twenty-something mama.

Tiff opened the door with a sleeping Charlene cradled on her shoulder. She looked harried, as I thought any new mother would. Her hair was barely combed and tied in a loose ponytail, she wore no makeup and had circles under her eyes: not dark, just enough to give evidence of her lack of sleep. She was wearing sweatpants and a baggy blue sweater.

"Hey, you guys," she said and took a step back. "C'mon in."

"You look a little tired," said Nancy.

"Charlene's got the croup," said Tiff. "I haven't slept for a while."

"I'm sorry to hear that," I said. "Is that common?"

"Common enough. I go with her to Mom's when Bert's working, but I still have to get up with her."

"Oh. Is Bert working?"

"He's on duty tonight. He works most nights. I think it may be to get out of the house, but he says he gets more money working the third shift. Anyway, right now he's on-line at the bookstore with that guy from Charlotte. He starts his new job in March and he's getting a jump on things."

"Smart," said Nancy. "At any rate, come March, he won't have to work nights."

Tiff nodded. "You want to sit down?"

"Sure," I said, mostly for Tiff's sake rather than our own. She was bouncing Charlene now and the baby was beginning to stir.

I was right about the house, although it was in disarray, Tiff's housekeeping skills not keeping up with the baby's crouping skills. It was all the modern couple could want, wrapped up in a cute arts and crafts package. We sat on an uncomfortable sofa from Ikea after moving a stack of magazines to the matching coffee table.

"There's really no easy way to approach this, Tiff," I said.

"I know about Bert's affair," she said. "I've known about it since Christmas."

"Oh," I said, waiting for more.

"A well-meaning woman from the church gave me a call."

"Iona Hoskins."

Tiff sped up Charlene's bouncing. "I suppose. I didn't get her name."

"You know why we're here then," I said.

"Bert didn't kill that woman."

"He was being blackmailed," Nancy pointed out. "He doesn't know that you know. Why didn't you tell him?"

"I didn't know he was being blackmailed," said Tiff. "It was before Charlene was born. I guess I just didn't want him to ... to ..." She started to tear up.

"Never mind," said Nancy.

"Anyway," said Tiff, composing herself. "I still haven't told him I know. He'll tell me in his own time I guess."

"I gotta ask, Tiff. Where were you the morning that Bert interviewed for the job? It was a week ago Monday."

She looked puzzled, then startled when she realized what we were asking. She scrunched up her face, thought for a bit, then brightened slightly. "I was at the pediatrician from nine till eleven-thirty. Then Charlene and I went to lunch with mom and her friend Harriet in Blowing Rock — that place on the corner down from the church. I can't remember the name. I didn't get back to town until three or so. You can check with them."

"Okay," I said. "Thanks, Tiff. Will I see you tonight? The Ash Wednesday service?"

"I doubt it." She bounced Charlene a little harder, but it didn't help. The baby woke with a yowl.

"Come back to choir when you can," I said. "We miss you."

"I miss you guys, too," she said sadly.

*　*　*

"Why do you think she stays with him?" asked Nancy. "I'd toss that low-life out quick as a snake in a ..." she paused, thinking. "Eh, I'm not so good with metaphors."

"Similes, you mean," I said. "Quick as an Irishman on a double-date, quick as a combustible hedgehog in a match factory, quick as the upstairs maid in the johnny closet."

"What does that even mean?" asked Nancy, looking at me as though I'd lost my tiny mind.

"Nothing. That's the beauty of similes. You can just make them up and people will pretend you know what you're talking about. Quick as a gluten-free junebug."

"Quick as a snake in the ... uh ... garage. Being chased by a guy with a shovel."

"That's gonna take some work," I said. "You could go with 'quick as a snake in a toilet bowl,' or 'quick as a snake in a mousery.' Either of those will work."

"There's no such thing as a mousery."

"Sure there is. It's a nursery for baby mice. A snake would love it."

"Anyway, I'd toss his sorry butt out."

"I suspect there's some guilt hanging around about Bert's first wife. Then, the realization that, unless they do get married, Tiff has a baby to raise alone."

"Yeah, I guess. But Bert's not going to be a good and faithful husband, if past behavior is any indication."

"I expect you're right," I said.

Nancy's phone went off with a series of dings. She looked at the screen, flicked at it a few times, then said, "There's an email from some guy from India. Probably wants you to send five thousand dollars because his uncle is the long lost Maharajah and you could stand to make millions. It has an attachment. Want me to delete it from the server?"

"Is it from Dr. Neeraj Agrawal?"

"How did you know?"

"Don't delete it!"

"Okay, okay. Who is he?"

"The foremost expert on decoding computer ciphers."

"Really?"

"In this county anyway. We'll open it at the station."

I turned on the stereo in the truck. Before this evening's Ash Wednesday service, I intended to finish listening to *Ich bin der Welt abhanden gekommen,* my favorite of Gustav Mahler's orchestral settings of the poems of Friedrich Rückert. I always found it helpful to get in a gloomy frame of mind before this service and even by Mahler's standards, this song is magnificently morose. The opening lines say it all:

I am lost to the world with which I used to waste so much time. It has heard nothing from me for so long that it may very well believe that I am dead!

I had many recordings of this one, but no one has topped baritone Dietrich Fischer-Dieskau's performance. This was required listening on Ash Wednesday.

Nancy usually didn't mind listening to my selections when we drove around, or at least didn't complain much. In my humble opinion, her knowledge of music had advanced considerably over the years. She even appreciated the likes of Stravinsky and Benjamin Britten.

"Gloomy," she announced.

"Right," I said. "Now get on the phone to Kent and see if there's some test he can do for gluten intolerance."

A moment later she had him on the speaker. "Hi Kent," said Nancy. "You're on speaker. Hayden wants to know if you can do some test for gluten intolerance on Sabrina Bodkin."

"I still have the body, if that's what you mean."

"What about a test?" I asked.

"If she has celiac disease I can confirm by doing a test, but she has to have consumed some gluten. I'll have to do a biopsy of her small intestine to confirm the disease."

"I can confirm that she has eaten gluten. It was her last meal."

"Pete's pancakes," added Nancy.

"I'll get it started."

"Another question," I said. "If she was indeed a Celiac, would eating gluten cause her to pass out?"

"I gotta check on that one. Hang on a minute."

We listened to the sounds of a delicious English horn solo at the end of the song, then Kent came back onto the phone. "It looks like different people react differently depending on the severity of the condition, but if Sabrina Bodkin hadn't consumed gluten for several years and her system was all of a sudden inundated by it, it certainly could cause her to lose consciousness, maybe for several hours, until it worked its way out of her system. Not to mention, she'd be very sick."

"She probably wouldn't have died though," I said.

"Probably not."

"Okay, thanks. Could you call me back when you get a firm diagnosis?"

"Will do," he said, and rang off.

* * *

We walked into the station just as Dave was hanging up the phone.

"We have to go," he said, grabbing his coat. "Right now!"

"What's up?" I said.

"That was Ellie Darnell. The Blueridge Ladies of Murder are up at her place. They have Coogan Kilgore trapped in the barn and are threatening to shoot him."

"Ah, sheesh," I said, heading for the door with Nancy right behind me.

Nancy jumped in my truck, and Dave followed right behind in his car. Twelve minutes later we were close to Ellie's address, but we didn't know what we were looking for. Fortunately, Nancy spotted the mailbox at the bottom of the drive with the number painted on the side. The driveway was winding and led up into the woods. We drove up to the single-wide trailer that had seen better days. It was from the '70s probably, and was light yellow, sitting beside a large fallow garden. A bank of solar panels faced south, the wires running up a pole and directly into the trailer. There was a chicken yard adjoining the trailer and the chickens were against the back fence by the coop, huddled together and clucking. Some goats were milling around nervously.

As we were getting out of the cars, we heard a gunshot, then another. I saw three more vehicles, further away from the trailer than we were, and I recognized one of them as Helen's SUV. Another shot.

Ellie had been on the wooden stoop in front of the door. Now she ran across the gravel drive to meet us.

"They're down there," she screeched, pointing down a long, grassy hill toward a large barn, a structure that predated the trailer by about fifty years.

Dave jumped into the back of the truck, I put it into four-wheel drive, and we headed toward the barn, about two hundred yards away. Nancy had her Glock out, and had reached into the pistol safe under the seat and gotten mine out as well. Dave was defenseless, except, of course, for his charm and boyish good looks.

In front of the barn, were the members of BLaM, well, five of them: Helen Pigeon, Pammy McNeil, and the three ladies who worked at the Piggly Wiggly, Hannah, Amelia, and Grace. All three of the older women had pistols in their hands. Helen was screeching something, her hands held to her face. Pammy was hanging back, looking scared.

I stopped the truck, laying on the horn, and jumped out yelling for everyone to put down their guns. In reply, Amelia let loose a barrage of four shots aimed about head-high right into the closed barn door.

"I give up!" came a voice from inside. It was answered by Hannah and Grace, each firing three times into the old wood. Splinters flew and the shots echoed across the valley.

"Drop your weapons!" barked Nancy, running up behind the ladies, her own gun in a two-handed grip.

"Right now!" I yelled, my gun up as well. "You're all under arrest!"

All the women spun around at this unexpected development, the three guns still in hand.

I pointed my Glock at Amelia. "Drop that gun right now or I will shoot you, Amelia, and I'm not kidding."

Her mouth dropped open and the gun fell from her twitching fingers.

I swung around toward Hannah and Grace who were standing together, but Nancy already had them in her sights and they were just as scared. Their two Berettas fell to the ground as one.

"Don't shoot!" cried Helen. "We have the killer captured!"

"Helen," said Nancy, furious, "I swear to God ..."

"It's that Coogan fellow," said Helen, breathlessly. "We figured it all out. He was having an affair with Sabrina Bodkin and then he found out that she was having an affair with Bert Coley, the sheriff's deputy. It was a crime of passion!"

Dave collected the three guns and put them on the hood of the truck. Then he walked back over to the barn.

"And what led you to that conclusion?" I said to Helen.

"Well, once we discovered that he was one of the duck people that was in St. Germaine that morning, it was easy. We just asked around."

"Asked around where?" Nancy asked.

"Around town. Angelique, at the post office, said she saw him walk by Sabrina's car that morning just before she was killed."

"She said maybe," said Pammy, correcting her. "That was after we showed her a picture."

"Because he was parked two cars in front of Sabrina," I said. "Where did you get a picture anyway?"

"Off the internet," said Hannah. "He has a website. Did you know he is an *actor*?

"Can I come out now?" called a voice from inside the barn. "Is it safe?"

"C'mon out," I called back.

"Are you guys the cops?" yelled the voice.

"Yes!"

"Get this!" whispered Helen. "He has a degree in chemistry. Chemistry! He would absolutely know how to poison someone."

"Probably," said Dave, "but Sabrina was strangled."

"*After* she was knocked out," said Helen. "See, here's the way it went down. Coogan was having an affair with Sabrina, then found out she was sleeping with Bert on the side. He comes with her to St. Germaine to talk her into coming back to him, but she says, no, she's in love with Bert. Coogan, in a fit of jealous rage, slips her a mickey, then strangles her with the nearest object, the umbilical cord from the rubber baby."

"We spotted him in town," said Grace. "We were having our meeting at the Ginger Cat and I saw him walking on the sidewalk. He got into his car and took off."

"So we all jumped in our cars and followed him out here," said Amelia. "We knew it was the killer. All the evidence pointed right to him."

"We knew it had to be a man, you see," said Pammy. "We read that on the internet. If it's a strangler, it's usually a man."

"We had him cornered," said Hannah ruefully. "Now we won't even get credit for the bust."

"How do you know it was Coogan Kilgore? What about the other man in the Friends-of-Ducks group?" asked Nancy. "What about Halbert Grayson?"

"He had a skin tight alibi," said Helen. "We found out that he was in Paris on that morning."

"No," said Dave, "he was parked behind the library and left at the same time the rest of them did."

"He did?"

"Helen," I said, "he was in the Slab, having breakfast with the others."

"He was?" She thought a moment, then, "Oh."

"I'm coming out," called the voice. "Don't shoot!"

"C'mon out," I called again, then turned to Helen and the others. "You do know that Coogan Kilgore is gay, right?"

"What?" said Helen.

"He's gay. He wasn't having an affair with Sabrina, so it wasn't a crime of passion."

"He's gay?" said Amelia. "A good looking boy like that?"

"Take them over to the truck," I said to Dave. "We'll have them follow us back to town, then book them."

"Book us?" said Helen. "What on earth for?"

Dave whistled and said, "Let me count the ways ..."

The barn door swung open and Coogan Kilgore came out, gingerly and slowly, looking around for armed vigilantes.

"They could have killed me!" he said. "They were shooting for my head!"

"We figured you'd duck," muttered Amelia. "We were just keeping you pinned down."

"Go to the truck!" I said, and the ladies started to move. "Coogan, over here with me." I motioned to Nancy to come with us.

I led Coogan several paces away, then asked, "Why'd you come out here?"

"I had business to talk to Ellie about," he said. "I was on my way home from an audition at the university. I thought I'd swing by and we'd get some dinner. I called from town and she gave me directions."

"We should get some pictures," said Nancy. "At least of the barn doors. They shot them up pretty good."

"Yep," I said. "Go ahead." I heard a phone ring behind me. Dave's phone.

"Then what?" I asked Coogan.

"We were standing on the porch getting ready to drive over to Jewell's for dinner and these crazies drive up, jump out of their cars, and start waving guns. I was sort of laughing, but then they started yelling my name and shooting. Ellie just stood there in shock. I didn't ask any questions, I just took off. Then as I was going down the hill, I saw the barn and thought it was my best chance."

"Then they trapped you in there," I said.

"They kept yelling that they knew I killed Sabrina and I might as well admit it."

"But you didn't."

"No, I didn't kill her."

"I mean, you didn't admit it," I said with a smile.

"That either. There's something you should know, though. I was gonna call you. I found something."

Then came a shot and everything seemed to happen in slow motion. I spun toward the sound and saw all three of the Piggly Wiggly checkers holding their guns, waving them around, more or less in our direction, seemingly in a panic. Dave was two steps away, his back having been turned, talking on his cell phone, now he was lunging at the trio. I saw Nancy in my periphery, caught totally off guard, making a grab for her own holstered gun. Helen and Pammy were standing off to the side of my truck, expressions of horror on their faces. An interminable second later, Dave plowed into the three old ladies knocking them down. The three guns flew into the air and fell to earth.

My sense of time and place returned to normal in an instant. "Dave? You okay?"

"I'm okay. My fault. Sorry. That was a call from 911 dispatch checking on the situation."

"Nancy?"

"Okay," said Nancy.

I turned to Coogan, but he was looking at me with a blank expression. I looked down at his front and saw a red stain spreading across his shirt, chest high, left of center. He stared at me for another second, then fell over backwards.

"Dave, help me get him in the truck," I yelled. "Nancy, collect those guns and get these women in jail."

The ride to the hospital was fast and nerve-wracking. Coogan was wedged in between us, sitting on the seat, his chin resting against his bloodstained chest. I didn't see any sign of a breath. Dave was calling the hospital before we even got off the property and they assured us they would be waiting at the emergency room entrance when we arrived. Still, with the ice on the back roads and me doing my best not to kill us all, it was close to twenty minutes before we saw the ambulance entrance sign. I drove up fast and slammed on the brakes, stopping with a squeal of rubber against pavement. The medical staff had Coogan out of the truck, onto a gurney, and into the hospital quicker than I managed to get out of the pickup. I sat down in a heap on the sidewalk, exhausted, not so much from the effort of wrestling Coogan into the truck and driving like a maniac, but from the stress of the situation. I thought again of my daughter and wondered if this was worth it.

"You okay, Chief?" Dave said, sitting down next to me.

"Yeah, I'm okay." I took a deep breath. "Coogan's not going to make it, is he?"

"I doubt it. To tell you the truth, I thought he was dead when we put him in the truck."

"Man," I said, shaking my head. "You did good, keeping pressure on his chest."

"It was my fault," said Dave. "I got that call from 911 and turned my back. I never thought they'd grab the guns, much less shoot."

"I'm sure it was accidental," I said, "but that's not going to save them this time."

"They could have hit you just as easily. You were standing right beside him."

"I'm aware."

"What about Helen and Pammy?" Dave said.

"Depends what the D.A. wants to do, I guess. Would you go back in there and make sure the doctors get that slug to the ballistics folks at the Boone Police Department?"

"Sure," said Dave, and he left me sitting on the sidewalk in the cold.

Chapter 20

"Where have you been?" hissed Georgia. "The service started fifteen minutes ago."

I'd come in the doors that led to the narthex and was now standing at the back of the church.

"I've had a bad afternoon," I said. "What's going on?"

"What's going on is this," Georgia said. "Father Jim is in the hospital in intensive care."

"What? When did this happen?" I was truly shocked at the news.

"About an hour ago. Dorothy called this morning and said he was feeling worse and couldn't do the service this evening. Then she called back at lunch time and said he was better and would be here." Georgia took a deep breath.

"And then?"

"And then she calls an hour ago and says that they've just gone to the hospital. Then she calls again, and now he's in intensive care."

"We probably just missed them," I said.

"Why?" asked Georgia, alarmed. "What were you doing at the hospital? Meg's here. I saw her."

"Nothing to do with Meg or the baby. I'll tell you later. Then what?"

"Then I called Father Tony, but he's in South America for a month doing some mission thing."

"I remember he told me about that."

"So now we have a service and no priest."

"Well, the imposition of ashes isn't exactly a sacrament. At, least I don't think it is. Did you get someone to do it?"

"Baylee Trimble," said Georgia.

My eyebrows went up into my hairline.

"She was the only person around that I could find. Bev's in Lenoir. You weren't available. Baylee said she'd do it."

"Why didn't you do it?"

"No way," said Georgia, and made a face. "Anyway, the choir showed up to sing, but when you weren't here, they just went down and sat in the congregation. Marjorie played the opening hymn on the piano. So far Baylee's doing fine …"

"Correct me if I'm wrong, but Baylee didn't exactly grow up in the Episcopal Church, did she?"

"Nope, but it's not that hard. You just read the service right out of the book."

"Okay."

"I told her just do what the priest did last year. Say what's in the book, make the sign of the cross with the ashes. Blah, blah, blah, nothing to it."

"Nothing to it," I agreed.

"Hey," said Georgia, looking up to the front of the church. "Baylee's coming to the altar rail. It's time for the ashing."

"All right," I said, "I'll go first then go up to the loft and play some holy ashing music. You come with me."

"Yeah," said Georgia. "Okay."

I signaled to the ushers, Billy Hixon and Calvin Denton, and walked with them up to the front. They waited by the first pew, then, when Georgia and I were kneeling, sent the congregants in the first row to join us.

Baylee was dressed in one of the white acolyte robes with a white cincture. She'd finished with the hard part, the salutation and collect, the readings, Psalm 51, and the rest. Now she stood in front of us holding a small bowl, presumably filled with ashes of some kind. At St. Barnabas, it was never a good idea to ask where the ashes came from. She had no book, however, one hand holding the bowl, and the other getting ready to impose the ashes upon our collective foreheads.

"She knows the blessing, right?" I said, under my breath.

"How should I know?" Georgia muttered back, but her head was bowed and she wasn't looking up.

I was looking up, though, and Baylee came to me first. She dipped a finger into the bowl, came up with a blackened digit (so far so good, I thought), drew the sign of the cross on my forehead and said very loudly and clearly:

> *"Look upon our Savior,*
> *Be on your best behavior,*
> *Ashes, ashes, we all fall down."*

Georgia's head came up like she'd been poked with a cattle prod, eyes wide, panic in her face. Baylee took it as a sign to continue her ministrations on Georgia's forehead.

"Look upon our Savior,
Be on your best behavior,
Ashes, ashes, we all fall down."

"Moosey," I thought with a smile, then got up and walked stoically down the side aisle toward the choir loft stairs in the back. I'd heard him chanting the rhyme last year during the Ash Wednesday service. "Be on your best behavior," I said, to no one in particular, and climbed the stairs to the organ bench.

Strangely, and most probably because everyone was busy praying for Father Jim, there wasn't much laughter and Baylee Trimble never knew she'd gotten it wrong.

I managed to deftly work *Ring Around the Rosie* into my improvised organ meditation while the rest of the congregation got smeared with ashes. Baylee was not adroit at making the sign of the cross and most of the congregation ended up looking as though someone had squashed a large black spider on their heads, a few of them resembling members of Seal Team Six, all camoed up for a night raid. We finished the service, sang *Forty Days and Forty Nights*, and headed out into the cold, cold evening.

Meg and I drove home in her Lexus and I left the truck at the police station. "Be on your best behavior," she said. "Not bad advice for Lent."

"It's too late for the Blueridge Ladies of Murder," I said, then told her what happened earlier in the afternoon.

"You could have been killed," she said.

"Yes, I could have. I've been thinking about just that all evening."

"I guess, as a police officer, you could be killed anytime," she said.

"Any of us could die tomorrow. We are not guaranteed anything. This job is about as safe as any job I could have. I've only ever been shot at twice. Once by that crazy priest's wife, and now today."

"And today they weren't really shooting at you."

"No, they weren't. I think it was an accident. All three of them looked stunned when it happened."

"Are they still in jail?"

"I would say the answer is yes, unless Jeff managed bail for Helen and maybe Pammy. It's late though and he might not be able to get a judge until tomorrow morning. Amelia, Hannah, and Grace won't be getting out for a while longer."

"You'll call when we get home and find out?"

"Sure I will."

* * *

I called Nancy once we'd gotten home and got the lowdown. Coogan Kilgore had managed to survive the night, thanks in no small part to the heroics of the trauma team at the hospital. He was in a coma, however, in critical condition, and the doctors told us that it was still touch and go. The three checkout ladies were locked up and charged with attempted murder. Helen and Pammy were charged with attempted murder as well, since we couldn't think of anything else at the time. Jeff Pigeon was in Raleigh and couldn't get back until the next morning. I wasn't feeling particularly charitable toward any of these five women and was happy for them to spend a night in the lockup. They would be there when Nancy and I went round to see them, first thing after breakfast.

"We have an interesting conundrum," said Nancy. "I've been thinking about it.

"Do tell," I said.

"I'll tell you tomorrow. See you at the Slab."

Chapter 21

Meg drove me into town the next morning as she was going with her mother into Boone for some last minute baby shopping. I couldn't imagine what this would entail, as we had accumulated everything a well-heeled baby would want, from a bluetooth baby video monitor to ergo baby mocs (as though the little tyke will be hiking the Appalachian Trail). I held my peace, kissed Meg goodbye, and bade her purchase whatever our little princess might require. Moments later I joined Dave, Nancy, and Pete at our usual table. Manuel was in the kitchen, Noylene was working the floor, there were a few customers, but the Slab wasn't full by any means. Pete didn't really rely on the Slab Café to make his monthly nut. Oh, it helped to be sure, but he had been an investor in the downtown St. Germaine real estate market for decades and now collected substantial rents from the businesses around the square. When he'd been mayor of the town, there had been several ordinances by the town council that came down in favor of property owners. Pete made no apologies.

"Here's the problem," said Nancy, sipping her coffee. "Coogan Kilgore was shot in the chest by one of three identical guns held by three old ladies. But which one?"

"Aha," I said. "I see where you're going with this."

"I don't," said Pete. "Explain it."

"We didn't see which gun went off," Nancy said, "but obviously one did. Then Dave spun around and dove into the bevy of old ladies ..."

"To save the chief," said Dave.

"For which I am heartily grateful," I said.

"Dave dove into them," continued Nancy, "and took them all down. The guns were knocked out of their hands and landed on the ground."

"Okay," said Pete.

"The problem is, we can't tell which one of the ladies actually pulled the trigger. Of course, they're all denying it."

"What about your forensic bullet guy?" asked Pete.

"We have the bullet and we can certainly match it to one of the guns," I said, "but we don't know which lady had which gun. They were all on the hood of the truck, then snatched up when Dave's back was turned."

"They don't know their own guns?"

"Well, I can't tell the difference. I don't know how they could. They all appear identical except for the serial numbers. They're all Berettas, all automatics, all black with the exact same grips. They bought them from Dr. Ken's Gun Emporium. They all ordered them at the same time, and got identical weapons. When we test the bullet, we can identify who the murder gun is registered to, but we still don't know who fired it."

"Gunshot residue?" asked Pete.

"They all had it on their hands," Nancy said. "They'd been shooting up the barn like they were at the O.K. Corral."

"This sounds like a defense attorney's dream case," said Pete. "There will always be reasonable doubt."

"Unless the state tries them all together and convicts all three," I said.

"Can they do that?" asked Pete.

"Yep," I said.

"That seems harsh."

"I expect that Judge Adams will say that as well," I said.

"What about Helen and Pammy?" Pete asked.

"We're going to see them after breakfast. I expect that Jeff will get them out of jail by nap time."

"Speaking of breakfast," Dave said, "I could go for some of those gluten-free pancakes."

"Yeah," said Pete, getting to his feet. "I'll get right on that."

* * *

"You gotta get us out of the Big House!" cried Grace. "We won't last a day in here."

"You shot Coogan Kilgore," I said.

"It was an accident!" yowled Amelia. "We just wanted to get our guns back. You know how much they cost us?"

"I expect that you're about to find out," said Nancy.

"It wasn't one of us," said Hannah. "We wouldn't ever shoot anyone."

"You shot those boys back a few years ago," I said. "They were on your porch on Halloween dressed as zombies. Remember that?"

"Oh, that doesn't count," huffed Hannah. "Anyway, that was with a shotgun."

"You shot Bennett Shipley in the Piggly Wiggly. All three of you."

"He was dressed as a gorilla," said Grace. "And we had a gorilla hunting license."

"You shot poor Mr. Hopkins when he forgot to pay for his groceries," Nancy said.

"That was a righteous shoot," said Amelia defiantly. "Nobody steals a can of Green Giant Niblets and gets away with it! Not on our watch!"

"He had Alzheimers," Nancy said. "You just got lucky with the judge. Not this time, though."

"You shot that Jehovah's Witness last fall," I said. "Right at your front door. You'd have killed him, too if your bullet hadn't lodged in his Bible. You scared him into becoming a Presbyterian."

"He shouldn't have rung the doorbell during Final Jeopardy," said Amelia. "Anyway, I sure didn't shoot that Coogan guy."

"Me, neither," said Grace. "My finger wasn't even on the trigger."

"It wasn't me," howled Hannah. "I have to get home and feed the cats."

"Where are Helen and Pammy?" I asked.

"The screws came and got them about fifteen minutes ago," said Grace. "I guess they're going to waterboard them or something."

"We'll talk to you later," I said.

"Wait!" cried Amelia. "Don't leave us in the hoosegow!"

"The Black Hole of Calcutta," sobbed Hannah.

"We'll never survive in Stoney Lonesome," wailed Grace. "We'll have to become some giant lesbian's bitches!"

We left them in their nice little cell and wound our way through the corridors to the sergeant's desk. There, standing in front of the counter, were Helen and Jeff Pigeon, and Pammy McNeil. Jeff turned when he saw me and Nancy, and walked over.

"Heck of a thing," he said.

"It is," I said.

"Helen and Pammy didn't have anything to do with it."

"They were there. They were part of it. They had no business chasing that man into the barn with guns."

"They didn't have the guns," said Jeff.

"No, they didn't," I agreed. "I'm sure the district attorney will consider that."

"We didn't do anything wrong," insisted Helen. "I was trying to get those ladies to put their guns away, wasn't I, Pammy?"

"She was!" said Pammy, nodding her head. "Me, too. We kept yelling at them to stop."

"You brought them out there, Helen. You knew they had guns in their purses. We all knew it."

Helen's shoulders slumped. "We were just trying to catch the murderer. I guess I never thought three old ladies would do such a thing."

"Don't say anything else," Jeff said, putting his hand on Helen's shoulder to stop her from talking. He looked over at me. "We'll have to get a lawyer, of course."

"Of course," I said.

"Judge Adams set Helen and Pammy's bail at five thousand dollars each. I just paid it."

"That sounds fair," I said. "These two certainly aren't a flight risk and Coogan Kilgore is still alive. If he dies, though ..."

"I know," said Jeff, raising both hands as if he could keep that eventuality from happening. "You know I'm running for the State Senate, right? This isn't going to do my campaign any good."

"Don't be too sure," said Nancy. "The way things are going in politics these days, Helen and the women of BLaM may be the heroes of the hour, especially if Coogan was involved in the other killings in some way."

Jeff brightened. "You think he was?"

"Nah," I said. "Not much of a chance, but you never know. It all depends on how you spin it. Alternate facts ..."

"Hey," said Nancy, "did the other three get their bail set?"

"Yeah," said Jeff, "but it's a lot higher since one of them was the shooter and the shooting happened during commission of a felony. One hundred thousand apiece, cash bond."

"They won't be getting out for a while," I said.

"Why weren't Kimmy Jo Jameson and Goldi Fawn with you?" Nancy asked.

"Kimmy Jo had to show a house up at Laurel Farms," said Pammy. "Goldi Fawn had an appointment for coloring and a reading at the Beautifery. She thought she might talk the gal into some essential oils, too. We were all having lunch together when we saw that Coogan guy, but then Kimmy Jo and Goldi Fawn said they couldn't come with us."

"Lucky for them," Nancy said.

"I'll say," said Helen. "Are you sure Coogan Kilgore wasn't the gunsel who rubbed out Sabrina?"

"Pretty sure," I said. "He was the first one of the Friends-of-Ducks to leave town. Sabrina was still alive, sitting in her car."

* * *

Driving the truck back to the station, I thought of something.

"You know what?" I said to Nancy. "Right before he got shot, Coogan said something to me. You were over by the barn taking pictures."

"Yeah? What'd he say?"

"He said there was something I should know, that he was gonna call me because he found something."

"Cryptic," said Nancy.

"Cryptic indeed," I said.

My phone rang and I handed it to Nancy. "It's Kent Murphee," she said, looking at the ID, then, "Hi Kent. This is Nancy. I'm in the truck with Hayden."

Kent's voice came over the speaker. "I have your answer I think. Sabrina Bodkin was definitely a Celiac. Her tTG numbers are off the chart."

"So Pete's pancakes might well have made her sick?" I asked. "Maybe even pass out?"

"I have no way of judging her body's reaction to an inundation of gluten, but I can say with confidence that she would have had some reaction. Probably quite a powerful one."

"There was no vomiting," I said. "Nothing else we could find, and you did the autopsy."

"Your theory is more than plausible. I can't tell you that it's a certainty that she *did* pass out, but I can tell you that she *may* have passed out."

"Thanks, Kent," I said. "Talk to you later."

"Have a blessed day," he said, a snigger lurking in his voice, and hung up.

Chapter 22

The nave of St. Mumford-Pancake was hububbing like a wattle of inebriated altar guild members. The baby cows loitered in the apse, mooing for their evening milk.

"Are you gonna feed those things, or what?" Pedro asked Tryxee. She hoisted her decoupage, but otherwise ignored him.

The Choralati, all twelve of them, dressed in their red capes and Mardi-Gras masks, lurked behind the squints, burning incense and singing campfire songs. Donald the Fig and the Big Schlemiel were squatting by the lectern with a couple of gunsels shooting craps. Stink-Eye Lewis and Jimmy Snap were busy looting the wine cupboard.

The contestants of the Dittersdorf Competition were in the choir loft, busy injecting steroids into their vocal cords and singing Dudley Buck art songs, each one trying to out-cadenza the next. Bassington was going through the trash can looking for enough used communion doilies to make a scarf.

"I told you my name is Gerald!" he yelled.

"Shut up, Bassington!" Pedro hollered back.

The Extremely Reverend Biff Wellington was propped up in the bishop's chair exhibiting much the same personality as he had in life, unnoticed by the coppers who were walking the beat in the transepts twirling their billies. Ermentrüde walked up and down the center aisle serving drinks, and Rex the famous detecting dog had cornered a wayward deacon in the aumbry.

"That seems to be everyone," I said.

"What about the beautiful yet mysterious Moldavian woman?" asked Pedro.

"She's in the confessional," said Tryxee, appearing on my arm, "because the bathroom was locked."

"So, solve the case," said Pedro.

"Solve the case! Solve the case!" the crowd chanted.

I ascended the pulpit like Martin Luther in 1517 ready to condemn the practices of Rome, wondering if my pronouncement was going to end as badly and if there might be tuna casserole served later. I raised my arms for quiet.

"Solve the case!" yelped Ermentrüde.

"Solve the case!" the crowd echoed. "Solve the case!"

"Here's the thing," I hollered back. "There is no case. There never has been a case."

The crowd fell silent and looked around at each other puzzledly. Even the baby cows looked confused.

"Well," said Pedro. "I never saw THAT coming."

* * *

Back at the station, Dave had opened the email from Dr. Neeraj Agrawal and printed it out. The first five pages contained the gibberish we'd found in the old guitar. The second five pages were readable.

"Dr. Agrawal has a note here at the top," Dave said. "Rot47 is a variant of Rot13, itself a variant of the Caesar cipher. The Rot47 cipher uses an alphabet that is a subset of the ASCII characters between character thirty-three and the character one hundred twenty-six. Rot47 replaces a character with another located forty-seven positions after it in the alphabet."

"Great," I said, not understanding much of what Dave had just said, but remembering Dr. Agrawal's earlier explanation.

"Look here," he said. "Here's the first bit."

```
w2=36CE vC2JD@? d_[ _c`d`hea $$Rbdc\gec\__ab
#@FE:?8 }@] ceaghfebc p44E }@] ghecdab``a !9]
gagcbfhgcd |2DE6Cr2C5 agfegdbcadeh__gf 6IA _ha_`h
p>tlagefcdb`cefdgh_d 6IA _ca_`e {:?6@74C65:Eq2?
<@7p>6C]aacbhefade 'x$pg___hefcbegefc`a6IA`aa_`f
w@>66BF:EJ agf_hdech_
```

"Now, here's the same stuff, decoded."

Halbert Grayson 50, 04151962 SS#354-864-0023 Routing No. 462897634 Acct No. 8964523112 Ph. 8284379845 MasterCard 2876853425690087 exp 092019 AmEx2867453146758905 exp 042016 Lineofcredit BankofAmer.2243967256 VISA8000967436867412exp122017 Homeequity 2870956490

"Well, that's that then," said Nancy. "All his information. Who else is on there?"

Dave perused the first page. "There are some names, but no pertinent information that I can see. Here's someone named Sidney Putnam, then Patsy Cobb, Esme Leighton, Norm Hooper, Abram Irving, Kennedy Munson."

"Future marks, maybe?" I said.

"Maybe. Here's what looks like a list of credit card numbers and expirations, but with no names attached. She might have skimmed them somewhere."

"Then sells them," said Nancy.

"Could well," agreed Dave. Then, "Ah. Here's Jared Fish's name with 10K behind it. Bert Coley's is next. It has 10K behind it as well, and another note, DigiZoot 301."

"That's when Bert starts working for DigiZoot," I said. "First of March. He said Sabrina had other plans for his blackmail since he didn't have the cash."

"Someone named Kerr Durant, then Tyler Porter, and Mason Ainsworth."

"Busy girl," Nancy said.

"This file goes back aways," said Dave, flipping past pages. "Four, no five years."

He turned back to page two. "Hang on," he said. "Here's something. Ellie Darnell."

"Ellie?" said Nancy. "What does it say?"

"It doesn't," said Dave. "Nothing except a date. December 6, 1993."

"A date that will live in infamy," I said.

Bev burst into the station, her face white.

"What?" I asked. "What's happened?"

"Father Jim," Bev said, her voice cracking. "He's dead."

* * *

Bev and I walked across the park to the church, and she filled me in on what she knew. Father James Hook had been admitted to the hospital yesterday afternoon. By six o'clock he was in intensive care. At one this afternoon, he died.

"What on earth happened?" I asked.

"Dorothy called Marilyn this morning. She said that it was something called ARDS."

"I've never heard of it."

"Acute Respiratory Distress Syndrome," said Bev. "They had him on a ventilator this morning, but then he had a heart attack around noon. They pronounced him dead an hour later."

"Who's at the hospital?"

"Georgia is over there. Father Tim, Baylee Trimble ... I think there are a bunch of folks from the church. I'm on my way over there now."

"I'll drive," I said.

* * *

On the way over, I called Meg and gave her the sad news. She decided she'd come to the hospital as well. The weather hadn't broken and it was still bitterly cold, but there wasn't any snow or ice on the roads and her Lexus would handle the roads without a problem. I wasn't worried about Meg.

The waiting room at the hospital in Boone was a sorrowful place. There were about fifteen people surrounding Dorothy with more of our people coming in. She was haggard from lack of sleep. There were circles underneath her red-rimmed eyes. Her dark brown hair was unkempt, and she kept pushing unseen strands of it behind her ears, probably from stress. I made my way up to her and expressed my shock and sadness at Jim's unexpected passing.

"Please accept my deepest condolences. I can't imagine what you must be going through right now."

"Thank you, Hayden," she said. "Jim was so looking forward to working with you for many years. He said this was his dream job."

"I was looking forward to that, too," I said. "I would have liked to have known him better. I know it's hard, and when it's so sudden it adds to the grief, but know that you and your family are in all our prayers. If there's anything we can do ..."

"Thank you, Hayden," she said, and gave me a hug. I moved on and let the next comforter in line take my place.

I waited for Meg to arrive and by that time the waiting room was full of parishioners. I gave her a kiss, made sure Bev had a ride back to St. Germaine, then got in my truck and drove back to town, no music playing, my cell phone turned off.

* * *

I drove back to Ellie's place. It was important that I talked with her since we hadn't gotten the whole story when we'd first arrived. This was her account: the members of BLaM had shown up at her door, introduced themselves, and demanded that Coogan come out and surrender himself. Coogan came to the door and laughed at them, but then one of the old ladies pulled a pistol out of her handbag and he took off in the direction of the barn.

"You'll be glad to know that they're in jail," I said, when she'd finished her tale.

"Yeah. I'm glad."

"Could I trouble you for a glass of water?"

"Sure," she said and went to fetch it. She left me standing on the front stoop of her trailer, but came back to the door in a minute and handed me a tall glass of water.

"Thanks," I said, and took a gulp. "I need to look at Coogan's car. I'll be done in a jiffy."

"Okay," she said. "It's right beside the house, next to my pickup."

"You want to come along?"

"No thanks. It's too cold." She closed the door.

I walked around the side of the trailer, looked at Coogan's car, a white, older Chevrolet, then walked back to my truck. I opened the door, took out a cleaning rag from a box I kept in the back seat, and wrapped up the water glass, holding it carefully from the bottom in my gloved hand. Then I called Dave and told him to get a tow truck out to Ellie Darnell's place and pick up Coogan's Chevy.

Chapter 23

I dropped the glass at the station with instructions for Nancy to identify whoever's prints were on it.

"Who's are they?" she asked.

"Ellie Darnell's. Something else is going on."

"Want to share?" asked Nancy.

"She was on that list that we found in Sabrina's car," I said. "I was just out at her trailer. She's off the grid — an old truck probably bought with cash, large garden, solar power, chickens, and goats."

"So? We know those duck people are green."

"Why was she on the list? She has no credit cards, no loans, no boyfriend, no family we know about, nothing but a date. If she's on that list, it's a fair assumption that she's being blackmailed for something. Maybe she's not who she says she is."

"Makes sense. I'll run the prints."

"Where's Dave?" I asked.

"He went for a haircut. He said there was some more info from the computer printout, but he'd tell us after he got back."

"I'm going over to the Slab for a piece of pie. Run the prints and see what pops. You guys join me when he comes back."

"Will do."

* * *

The late afternoon was cold and sere and the sun dropped behind the bare trees, a fiery orange ball void of warmth. I walked the short distance from the station down the block to the Slab Café and banged on the front door. The Slab closed at 3:30, but Pete was still there, as were Noylene and Cynthia. I could see them cleaning the place up. Pete had the chairs up on the tables, upside down, legs in the air, and Noylene had her mop in hand, slopping suds across the linoleum floor. Cynthia, who was cleaning out the register, saw me first and tiptoed over to let me in.

"I need pie," I said. "Preferably apple, but I'll take peach in a pinch."

"And coffee?" asked Cynthia.

"Sure."

"Go away," said Noylene. "We's closed."

"I have money," I said. "Oodles and oodles of it."

Pete took the chairs off a table under which Noylene had already slopped and mopped and pointed me to it.

"We have rhubarb pie," he said, "or peach."

"Rhubarb, of course."

"Heated up, with some vanilla ice cream on top?"

"I'd be a fool to refuse," I said.

"Price is no object?"

"Right. As long as there's coffee."

"Coming right up," he said and went over to the dessert case.

Cynthia pulled up a chair and sat down next to me. "I heard about Father Jim. How's Dorothy?"

I shrugged.

"How are you doing?"

"I'm fine. You know, he's been at St. Barnabas for two months and I barely knew him. I mean, we had a few meetings, but I made no effort at all. I feel bad about that."

"It was Christmastime," said Cynthia. "Everyone's busy."

"Not an excuse," I said.

"That last priest was so bad. Kimberly Walnut was insane. You've had bad experiences with the clergy."

"Yeah. Still not an excuse."

"Meg's getting ready to have a baby," Cynthia offered.

I smiled. "Thanks. There's nothing I can do about it now, I suppose. When I left the hospital there were probably a hundred people in the waiting room consoling Dorothy and all of them knew Father Jim better than I did."

"Is that the reason for the pie? Is this self-pity pie?"

"Nope. This is thinking pie."

"Ah," said Cynthia. "So this is about the case."

"Yep."

Pete brought over three large slices of rhubarb pie, each topped with a scoop of vanilla ice cream. He set them on the table, then went to the coffee maker, got the pot and three cups, and managed to get back to the table without dropping anything.

"If this is thinking pie," he said, "you've got the case wrapped up."

"No, but Nancy's coming over with stuff that will help. Dave, too."

As if on cue, the door opened and the two police professionals walked in to the clanking of the cowbell against the glass.

"Hey!" shouted Noylene. "Just look at that floor! Now I gotta do the whole thing again! You take off your boots right now and leave them by the door!"

Dave and Nancy stuffed the papers they were carrying into their jackets, removed the offending articles, then walked gingerly across the still-damp floor to the table.

"Now my socks are wet," complained Dave, then his eyes lit up. "Is that rhubarb pie?"

"I'll have mine without ice cream," said Nancy. "It's Lent you know."

"I'll get it," said Cynthia with a laugh.

Dave and Nancy removed their coats and with them the papers they'd stuffed into the pockets.

"A couple of things," said Nancy, spreading her findings across the table. "I got a hit almost immediately on the fingerprints."

"Whose fingerprints?" asked Pete.

"Ellie Darnell's fingerprints." She turned to me. "You were right. Ellie Darnell isn't really Ellie Darnell. She's a woman named Cara Jenkins and there's a warrant out on her dating back to 1993 — second degree homicide in Wilmington. She was drunk, twenty-three years old, and caused an accident where an entire family was killed. Rather than face the music, she skipped bail and disappeared."

"December 6, 1993," I said.

"Exactly," said Nancy.

"Okay," I said. "So Sabrina and Bonnie found out about that somehow."

"How?" asked Nancy.

"My bet is that one of them got her talking at the Winter Solstice retreat. Their past selves, their future selves, their hopes, their dreams. Probably with some medicinal help."

"And then they blackmailed her."

"I think so, but Ellie, a.k.a. Cara, doesn't have much. A trailer and a beat up car, some chickens, and a few goats."

"If they found out about her right after the solstice, they've only been milking her for a couple of months," said Nancy.

"Yeah," I said. "What else?"

"The ballistic report came back on the bullet that shot Coogan Kilgore. It looks to be a .308 diameter slug, but they need the three guns before they can match the bullet to the barrel. You want me to get those guns over to ballistics?"

I shook my head. "Nope. Not just yet."

Cynthia returned with two more slices of pie, one à la mode.

"What have you got, Dave?" I asked.

He unrolled his papers and said, "A few more names near the bottom of the list. From about five years ago."

"Anyone we know?" asked Nancy.

"In fact, yes," said Dave. "Angelique Murray and Christy Maze. Complete personal information with social security numbers, bank account numbers, retirement account numbers, mortgages, loans ... the works."

"Oh, my word," I said, mostly to myself. "Mildred. Mildred the Bear."

"Hey, Dave," said Noylene, noticing Dave's freshly coiffured mop. "Nice haircut."

"I know, right?" said Dave. "Bill the Barber is great. Sorry Noylene, but I just can't go into the Beautifery."

"We don't do men," said Noylene. "They're too dang picky."

"I love Bill the Barber," said Pete. "I even went in for a shave just so I could have the hot towels and the Bay Rum."

"Is that what I smelled?" said Cynthia. "Bay Rum? I thought you'd been to a cathouse."

"He was telling me about Moosey," said Pete. "Says he offers him a couple of quarters or a dollar bill every time he comes in ..."

The room started to fade and I took a bite of my thinking pie. Mildred the Bear, Bonnie Pickering, Sabrina Bodkin, Moosey. I chewed slowly, savoring the tart bite of the rhubarb. Coogan Kilgore, Ellie Darnell. Then the fog lifted and it all became clear.

"Are you okay?" said Cynthia, waving a hand in front of my face.

"He's doing his detective thing," said Dave, diving into his piece of pie. "He'll come out of it in a bit."

"The day I take the dollar, the game is over," I said.

"Huh?" said Dave.

I told them all about Moosey's play for the quarters, then said, "It was right in front of us all along."

* * *

We finished our dessert, then I told Dave to go back to the office and call Judge Adams with a request for a search warrant.

"We won't serve it till tomorrow," I told Nancy, as we drove out to Ellie Darnell's place. "It's too dark tonight, but I want it in hand."

"What are we looking for?" asked Nancy.

"Well, for starters, we can arrest her on the outstanding warrant."

"Is there more?"

I nodded. "A lot more."

Chapter 24

By the time we got up to the trailer, the sun was setting and shadows were moving quickly across the narrow valley. I parked the truck in the front where I had before, then got out, walked up the steps, and knocked on the door. No answer. I knocked again.

Nancy was behind me and asked, "Where do you think she is?"

"Down at the barn. C'mon."

We walked across the field, two hundred yards, just in time to meet Ellie coming out of the barn, closing the big double doors behind her. She dropped a beam across a couple of iron brackets to secure them, then turned and saw us walking toward her. She froze for a moment, then steeled herself, put her shoulders back, and marched toward us, a strong woman, self-sufficient, used to living in the woods: a farmer, a hunter, someone who'd been in hiding for almost twenty years. She was wearing her old red parka and her red-plaid cap with the ear flaps down, heavy canvas trousers and insulated boots. Her face was red, from the cold or from exertion, I couldn't tell which.

"Yeah?" she said. "What do you need?"

"You're under arrest," said Nancy. "We have an outstanding warrant from 1993. Multiple homicides."

Ellie's face never changed. "I'm gonna need someone to watch my chickens and goats," she said.

"We'll send someone out tomorrow," I said.

"I might can beat that rap," Ellie said. "The case never went to trial. It could be that all that evidence is gone by now. Breathalyzer reports lost, all the cops dead or retired. Stuff disappears all the time."

"Maybe," I said, "but one thing is for sure. You'll be in jail tomorrow when we search your property."

Her eyes narrowed.

"I'm fairly confident that you're not going to beat *our* rap. The attempted murder rap. Or the vehicular homicide rap either."

Nancy looked at me, not quite with surprise, but with an eyebrow raised just a hair.

"The bullet they took out of Coogan was a .308, but the BLaM ladies were shooting Berettas. That's a .38 Caliber. They couldn't have shot him. You shot him from up here."

"You couldn't tell that was a .308 slug," said Ellie. "If I had shot him from up here, and I'm not saying that I did, that bullet would have been unrecognizable."

"Might have been," I said, "but Coogan was wearing a shirt, three sweaters, and a Melton wool overcoat. They not only saved his life, but also saved most of that bullet."

"Huh," said Ellie, blinking.

"Coogan told me something just before you shot him. He said he'd found something and was going to give me a call."

Ellie was silent.

"He found your car, didn't he? The one in the barn. The one that you used to run down Bonnie Pickering. The Subaru with the front end all banged up. Your pickup truck is up at the house, but your Subaru is gone."

"There's no car in the barn," said Ellie.

"No, I suppose not," I said, "but you haven't had time to move it far. I expect we'll find it in the woods somewhere, maybe down a ravine. The tracks will be easy to follow in the morning when it's light out. We'll also find the .308 rifle in your trailer and match the bullet to the gun. It won't be a problem."

Ellie's shoulders slumped. "You gotta promise to take care of my animals," she said.

"Sure."

She sighed heavily. "I knew Coogan would see that car and tell someone. I had no idea he'd run into the barn, for God's sake. I couldn't find my binoculars so I was watching you guys through the rifle scope and I saw him talking to you. Then, those crazy old bats picked up their guns and, well, I took the chance."

"Why'd you run down Bonnie Pickering?" Nancy asked.

"Bonnie and Sabrina used us," she hissed. "They were in it together. Cyndibeth Lee brought Sabrina to the Winter Solstice retreat and we ... well ... we got pretty high and were talking about stuff, you know. Sabrina was my star partner — we were both born on the Virgo-Libra cusp — and so I opened up to her. That's what the retreat is for, visiting our past selves, seeing our future selves ..." She trailed off, then, "Next thing I know this woman named Bonnie Wentworth shows up in the group and is demanding that I pay her five hundred bucks a month to keep quiet. I don't have five hundred bucks, but I sold some stuff and paid her off twice."

"Then Sabrina was killed," I said, "and Bonnie Pickering wanted a lump sum. She was ready to move on. I recognized her at the Slab as she was leaving."

Ellie nodded, rage still evident on her face. "Ten thousand. I don't got ten thousand and I don't got no way to get ten thousand!"

"The day I take the dollar, the game is over," said Nancy. "Bonnie got greedy."

"Yep," I said.

"Ten thousand seemed to have been a nice round number for them," Nancy said.

"It's a good number if you're a blackmailer," I said. "It's a lot, but not too much. Most folks, under major duress, can come up with ten thousand. Sell your guns, sell your car, a tractor, rob your retirement account, maybe steal some cash from work if you have to."

Ellie continued, "She said if I didn't get the money in a week, she was turning me in. I told her get in the car, I had the money at the house. Then I drove her up on Old Chambers, pulled out my H&K 9mm, and told her to get out and walk, I changed my mind and wasn't paying."

"So then you ran her down," said Nancy as she put the cuffs on her. "But how did you kill Sabrina? You were parked beside Hal at the library and you both left at the same time."

"I didn't kill Sabrina."

* * *

Choir practice was a somber gathering, the most downcast I had seen the choir since Muffy LeMieux had been electrocuted at the baptismal font while singing *On Eagle's Wings*.

"I had no idea it was that serious," said Rebecca finally, after I'd given the choir fifteen minutes to talk about Father Jim.

"None of us did," said Bev. "Not even Dorothy. Well, not until she got him to the hospital."

"We might as well rehearse," I said. "We have the Great Litany on Sunday and one anthem to sing."

"This anthem's going to be depressing, isn't it?" said Marty.

"Not too," I said.

"Can we sing something happy to start with?" asked Goldi Fawn. "How about *I've got the joy, joy, joy, joy, down in my heart*?"

"Nope," I said.

"How about *Deep and Wide*?"

"No."

She crossed her arms and glared at me. "*If you're happy and you know it, clap your hands*?"

"Look in your folders," I said, "and you'll find a copy of *Crossing the Bar*."

"I know the poem," said Elaine. "Alfred, Lord Tennyson, right? Have we sung this?"

"I don't think so," I said. "I just pulled it out of the old file cabinet. It'll work as an anthem on Sunday."

"So, we're not going to sing that mud song?" said Marjorie. "I was sort of looking forward to wallowing in that one." She was referring to Arlen Clarke's setting of the George Herbert poem, *Lord, who has formed me out of mud*, which, mud notwithstanding, was a beautiful anthem for the First Sunday of Lent.

"We're not singing the mud song," I said. "This will be better."

The members of the choir made themselves busy looking for the one page piece of music.

"It is Tennyson," I said, "with music by Hubert Parry. You remember Parry for his top-hundred hymn, *Jerusalem*, and his big coronation anthem, *I Was Glad*, but this is another one of his gems. Let's give it a try."

We did give it a try, and then we rehearsed it, and gave it another try, and another. Then we tweaked it, sang it a cappella, and it was lovely, just the right thing for Sunday.

> Sunset and evening star,
> And one clear call for me!
> And may there be no moaning of the bar,
> When I put out to sea,
> But such a tide as moving seems asleep,
> Too full for sound and foam,
> When that which drew from out the boundless deep
> Turns again home.

Twilight and evening bell,
And after that the dark!
And may there be no sadness of farewell,
When I embark;
For tho' from out our bourne of Time and Place
The flood may bear me far,
I hope to see my Pilot face to face
When I have crost the bar.

"Oh, wow," said Holly, wiping a tear from her face. I noticed she wasn't the only one.

"Will we be singing this at the funeral?" asked Phil.

"I don't know. I haven't heard anything about any arrangements," I said, and looked over at Bev.

"I haven't heard either," she said.

"Let's go downstairs and prepare for the Great Litany," I said. "Bullet, you'll be doing the canting."

"What does that mean?" he said.

"It means you're on the hot seat," said Randy Hatteberg. "I'm glad it's not me."

As the choir shuffled down the steps, I thought about the Great Litany in Procession, one of the traditions of St. Barnabas Church dating back to the stone age. I was told it was a tradition when I took the job, as was my predecessor, and his before him. On the First Sunday in Lent, the choir lines up behind the crucifer, the thurifer, and the cantor, followed by acolytes, the Gospel Bearer, lay ministers involved in the service, and the clergy, and winds its way around the inside of the church, dodging parishioners, children, wheelchairs, unruly ushers, and whoever else might be lurking in the aisles. Usually the priest served as cantor, but that would not be the case this coming Sunday. Our procession would march slowly around the church, once, twice, three times, answering the petitions of the cantor, all chanted, of course. It was fifty-fifty that the priest would get it right, but the choir was used to that and just kept right on going. The Great Litany in Procession took a full fifteen minutes and by the time we had finished, Benny Dawkins, the thurifer, would have created so much smoke in the building that if no one had remembered to turn off the fire alarms in advance, we'd be visited by the nearest three fire departments. This, along with having to cancel the service until the reset button could be found.

That's what we were preparing for, and now it was Bullet's turn in the spotlight.

"You're leading the procession, Bullet. First the crucifer ..."

"The what?" said Bullet.

I'd forgotten that Bullet was a Baptist by trade. "First in the procession," I explained, "is the crucifer — the person carrying the cross. Next is the thurifer. He's the guy who swings the incense pot. That will be Benny Dawkins and Addie Buss will be assisting. He's one of the top thurifers in the world. Addie's not far behind."

"You're in for a real treat," said Caroline Rollins. "Just make sure you keep your eyes on your music. Sometimes I get lost watching the smoke."

"Watching the smoke?" Bullet sounded confused.

"You'll see," said Caroline, smiling.

"You come next," I said, "then the choir and everyone else. You'll have to walk around the church a few times. It's a long litany."

"Sure," said Bullet. "Let's do it."

"Oh, and Bullet," said Marjorie sweetly, "you might want to change your hair to royal purple. It is Lent, after all."

Bullet gave her a smirk, and didn't seem to be perturbed by the comment. He might even take it to heart.

The choir circled the church, two-by-two, chanting as they went, Bullet in the lead.

"O God the Father, Creator of heaven and earth," sang Bullet.

"Have mercy upon us," replied the choir.

"O God the Son, Redeemer of the world," sang Bullet.

"Have mercy upon us."

Fifteen minutes and only a few mistakes later, we were finished, said a prayer, and headed home.

Chapter 25

"Solve the case!" the crowd yelled. "Solve the case!"

"Here's the thing," I hollered back. "There is no case. There never has been a case."

"What about the dead guys?" shimmied Tryxee. "The bishop and that guy you murdered? That should count as a case."

Suddenly a shot rang out, a woman screamed, and a bevy of angry nuns appeared in the vestibule, rulers at the ready. Somewhere in the back, a baby cried because that baby hadn't been taken to the nursery, even though the sign on the door clearly states that babies should be taken to the nursery.

A crack of thunder cracked ominously. A large black cloud appeared between the rafters, little lightning bolts flashing at the edges, and we could hear strains of the "Dies Irae" coming from the praise band speakers.

"Oh-oh," said Pedro. "We've seen this before, in Mexico. Remember the leprechauns? Let's take a powder."

* * *

The next morning I called the District Attorney in Boone and told him the situation. We agreed that the three Piggly Wiggly checkers would be with charged with reckless endangerment, a Class A misdemeanor, and the ladies would be released on their own recognizance since they didn't actually shoot Coogan. We'd keep their three pistols in custody as "evidence" until the case was decided. Helen and Pammys' bonds would be returned and the charges dropped.

Nancy, Dave and I were out at Ellie Darnell's place right after breakfast and served our warrant to no one in particular. Dave went ahead and stapled a copy to the front door, for good order's sake, immediately before we entered the single wide trailer to perform our perfunctory search, coming up with a Mossberg bolt-action .308, a Browning 12 gauge pump shotgun, and a Heckler & Koch 9mm semi-automatic pistol. Three guns, not an especially robust compilation of firearms, given that we were out here in the hollers. It was the .308 rifle we were interested in, but we took all three, then bundled up Ellie's computer, iPad, and phone. While we were in the trailer, the people from the animal shelter drove up and we showed them the livestock. They were busy rounding up chickens and goats and whatever else showed up as we made our way down to the barn.

There was snow in the forecast, but it was still a day away. The temperature was hovering around twenty degrees, depending where in the county you happened to be. Wherever you were, it was cold and likely to remain so. We opened the barn doors and looked at what could have been any barn interior in Watauga County. There were piles of old tobacco sticks, a vintage John Deere tractor with a bucket on the front, some spare tires, farm implements, tack, and livestock stores. There were bales of hay, ropes and pulleys hanging from hooks on the walls, buckets, shovels, rakes, and the like. There was one difference, though, one immediately obvious difference. Someone had swept every inch of the dirt floor, obliterating any marks that had been there. Leaning next to one of the center posts was a broom, the old-fashioned kind made of wood and straw. It wasn't hard to deduce what Ellie had been up to when we caught her yesterday.

"No tracks," said Dave. "She cleaned them all up."

"She can't have cleaned up those outside, Dave," I said. "It was too cold. The car tracks will have frozen into the ground. She needed a good thaw, or at least, a heavy snow. She got neither."

"Do we need any of these bullets that the old ladies shot into here?" asked Nancy. "The beams are peppered with them."

"I can't imagine that we do," I said, "but if so, we know where to find them."

"There are some back doors," Nancy said, pointing. "There, behind the tractor."

"They open from the other side," I said. "Let's take a walk."

We left the barn, then circled it, and didn't bother opening the back doors because we saw what we'd been looking for: two tracks, leading directly from the doors to the nearby woods. We followed them to the edge of the field, then into the trees, and along a narrow path for about a quarter mile, ending under a huge clump of laurels.

"Where is it?" asked Dave. "I sure don't see any car."

I ducked up under the big leaves, pushing them out of my face, then grabbed hold of a dark brown tarp and pulled it with me as I backed out of the underbrush. The tarp had been covered with dead leaves and the car and tracks would have been invisible when the snow fell.

Dave went into the laurel next, and began taking pictures of the front of the car.

"This is the one, all right," said Dave. "It's a ten year old Subaru Outback. There's a dent the size of a duck person, and blood frozen on the bumper and hood."

"Let's get the tow truck down here to haul it out," I said. "We have Ellie's confession, but we'll want this as well. "Get them to drop it down at the police lot in Boone. And make sure they keep it covered, will you? We don't need rain washing away any evidence."

"Will do," said Nancy, and got on her cell.

"Anything in the car?" I called to Dave, who had gotten the locked door open with his slim jim.

"She cleaned it out," said Dave. "There's not even a registration or a car manual in the glove compartment."

"We've got what we need," I said.

"What will happen to her property?" asked Dave, pushing his way out of the dense shrubbery.

"I don't know. The lawyers will get involved for sure if Coogan dies and has any next-of-kin. Same thing with Bonnie Pickering's family even though she was blackmailing Ellie. There will be lawsuits on lawsuits and it may take years. You can't kill people even though they're rotten."

When we got back to town, Nancy and I left Dave at the office to do the paperwork, and we headed to the Post Office.

"Why are we going over there?" asked Nancy as we walked across the frozen tundra that was Sterling Park.

"Something that Angelique said. Plus, she and Christy were on Sabrina's list. Near the bottom, but on it nevertheless."

"You think they were being blackmailed?" asked Nancy.

"I don't think so. Sabrina had all their personal information, but I didn't see anything on the list that might lead to blackmail."

We opened the post office door and walked into the lobby area, then up to the counter where Christy was sorting through some catalogs.

"Good morning," I said. "Is Angelique here?"

"I'll get her. I gotta go check on the boxes anyway."

"Just call her up, if you would," I said. "I need to talk to you both."

Christy shrugged and called, "Angelique! Come on up to the front, will you?"

A moment later, a back door opened and Angelique appeared behind the desk beside her partner.

"So, here's the thing," I said, getting right to the point. "Both of you were on a computerized list that Sabrina Bodkin had in her car. It was encoded and we had to get it all sorted out, but once, we did, there you were, big as Christmas."

Their smiles faded abruptly, but there was no panic in their faces.

"And?" said Christy.

"And, not only your names, but a whole lot of other personal information: both of your social security numbers, bank accounts, both your mortgages, both your retirement account numbers, and auto loans."

Christy and Angelique shared a quick look, then Christy said, "And?"

"And," I continued, "Sabrina, and her sister, Bonnie Pickering got into your life and your finances, and caused quite a mess. I already talked with the cops in Boone. They still have your complaints on file, even though nothing was done about it."

"Yeah," said Angelique, crossing her arms. "Nothing was done about it."

"You told me you were friends."

"We were," said Angelique.

"I'm thinking that Bonnie was the one who stole your information. Probably one of the times that she was subbing here in the post office."

Neither woman said anything, but now both of them had their arms crossed, defiant looks on their faces. Nancy stood by the counter, her hand on the butt of her pistol, but they couldn't see her hand, being behind the counter. I didn't see either one of these women making any kind of crazy move, but Nancy wasn't one to take chances. She smiled at them.

"See," I said, "Angelique mentioned that she hadn't thought of Mildred the Bear for years."

"So?" said Angelique. "I hadn't."

"None of us had. I looked it up. That bear has been dead since 1993. No reason to think about a dead bear, no matter how famous. That is, not until I saw that old bumpersticker on Sabrina's Pinto. You saw it, too, through the post office window that morning."

The women remained silent.

"You told us that you didn't notice any of the vehicles out front, but you sure noticed that bumpersticker. I think you recognized the car, either as Sabrina's or Bonnie's, maybe they even shared it back then. You hadn't seen either one, or even known they had returned to town." My eyes went from Angelique to Christy and back again. I said, "Sabrina dressed differently when she came in for the birthing classes and she was driving a Caddy. Bonnie never showed up at all till that morning when I recognized her at the Slab. You remembered the sticker though, and that old Pinto."

"Let me stop you right there," said Christy. "I'll tell you what we told the cops in Boone. Those two crooks stole our identities, stole our retirement money, wrecked our credit, cost us our houses, took out mortgages in our names, and left us both about a hundred thousand dollars in debt. They were a couple of lowlifes."

"Oh, I agree," I said, "but that's not a good enough reason to kill them."

"The police couldn't do anything about it," said Christy. "Or they said they couldn't. Not enough direct evidence. We got no money back and certainly didn't get the satisfaction of seeing them in prison."

"I can't say that we're sorry they're dead," said Angelique, smiling sweetly, "but we had nothing to do with it."

"You saw that bumpersticker," I continued, "then went outside and found Sabrina passed out in the front seat. The park was empty. It was cold and everyone was hunkered down inside. A quick look around to make sure you were safe, then a knot with a rubber umbilical cord, and it was over."

"She really was a horrible person," said Angelique.

"So which one of you did it?" I asked.

"I don't know what you mean," said Christy. "I was here all morning and I didn't see anything. I didn't even leave the post office. Cross my heart and hope to die. Angelique is my witness."

"I was right here as well," Angelique said. "We worked in the back till lunchtime since there wasn't any business. Well, except for that one time when Pete and Cynthia came in. Hmm ... now let me see ..." She gave me another delightful, one might almost say "angelic," smile. "I know what you want to ask. Do I have someone who can verify my whereabouts? Oh, yes! Christy can! We were both here the whole morning!"

"Indeed we were!" said Christy, brightly.

"Indeed you were," I said.

* * *

I went over to the church for Georgia's emergency worship meeting. It would have to be an emergency to get everyone there on a Friday afternoon, and there were several members missing. For instance, Meg had called to tell me she needed to stay home to rest. We were there to talk about Sunday's service. Since we were short a priest, we might be improvising on the First Sunday of Lent.

"Welcome to Lent," said Georgia, once the small assemblage had gathered around the conference table. "We have no clergy for Sunday. I called Bishop Varley's office and there are no supply priests available, so it looks like we're on for Morning Prayer."

"We haven't done Morning Prayer for ages," said Joyce Cooper.

"True," said Georgia, "but at least we can do it with Lay Readers." She looked over at me. "What do you think about our tradition?"

"We'll have to redo the bulletins, but I think we can still do the Great Litany. We don't need a sermon, and there's no communion. Mostly, it's readings and prayers. We should look at one of the Morning Prayer bulletins from a few years ago. No need to reinvent the wheel."

"How about music?"

"The congregation might sing one of the canticles, if we push them, but it's going to be easier on such short notice just to read them. The choir has an anthem they can do at the offertory."

"Is everyone on board for the procession?" Georgia asked.

"As far as I know," I said, looking around the table.

"The crucifer is ready," said Bev. "Acolytes and readers are raring to go. I talked to Benny Dawkins and he and Addie will be here."

"Bullet is the cantor," I said. "He's well prepared."

"Bullet?" said Baylee. "That's his name?"

"I know," said Marty, shaking her head. "It's hard to believe."

"He's a good cantor," said Caroline, "and his hair is easy to follow."

"Okay," said Georgia. "What could possibly go wrong?"

Chapter 26

"We're having lamb chops," said Meg from the living room. "What wine goes with lamb chops?"

"You're not having wine, dear," I said. I was in the kitchen cooking, and was discovering that I rather enjoyed it.

"I know," grumbled Meg, "but our guests are."

"Bud says we should have a Pinot Noir. It's classic. I stopped by the shop and got a couple of bottles."

"What kind?" asked Meg. She was a glutton for punishment, wanting to know what Bud had sent over, and knowing she wouldn't be having any. She had felt very guilty about her last lapse and had vowed it wouldn't happen again.

"It's called *San Andreas Fault* from Hirsch Vineyards, vintage: 2010." I said. "It's a fascinating tangle of Santa Rosa plums, sweet cherries, and a flutter of bitter tears from an unappreciated birthday clown. Spend an evening with a bottle and you'll discover you're in lust."

"You're reading that from a card, aren't you?"

"Yes, I am," I admitted. "I'm getting too old to remember this stuff. Sounds good though, doesn't it?"

"I guess," said Meg, glumly. "How's the dinner coming?"

"No problem," I said, meaning it. In truth, I was grilling the lamb chops but, while in town to get the wine, had also picked up a golden quinoa salad with lemon, dill, and avocado. The Ginger Cat was only too happy to oblige. Throw some bakery bread in the oven to warm up, add garlic butter, two kinds of cheeses, and the wine, and I was home free and dry.

Baxter was lying under the kitchen table, eyes on me, tail sweeping behind him like a hairy windshield wiper, watching for the moment when something hit the kitchen floor. With Meg it was a rare event, and usually she'd go ahead and drop something on purpose just to make him happy. With me, though, Baxter was playing the role of the canine vacuum cleaner. A slab of butter, a chunk of cheese, a raw egg, the wayward piece of avocado, even a bit of lamb chop, all these were hoovered up almost before they hit the ground.

The doorbell rang, then the front door opened and Pete's voice called out, "We're here. Everybody decent?"

"For heaven's sake," Meg called back. "I'm eleven and a half months pregnant, squatting on a footstool. How much more indecent can it get? C'mon in."

Cynthia and Pete came in and Meg met them in the kitchen.

"We brought cheesecake," said Cynthia, "but I'm not having any. I just tried to get into my belly dancing outfit and ... well ... let's just say that I won't be having cheesecake for the foreseeable future."

Meg harrumphed. "You're not getting any sympathy from me."

"I'm going to join that Pilates group at the church."

"I already signed up," said Meg. "Hayden's coming too."

"Wait," I said. "What?" I was busy turning the lamb chops, but now I was getting the gist of the conversation.

"Meg said that she's signing you up for *Paunches Pilates*," said Pete, grinning. "You'll have to get some yoga pants."

"You're coming as well," said Cynthia, pointing an accusing finger at Pete. "Just look at yourself!"

"Hey," said Pete. "I weigh exactly the same as I did in college."

"Except, over the last thirty-five years, about twenty pounds of that has dropped down a couple of feet," said Cynthia.

"I'm thinking about embracing suspenders as a lifestyle option," I said. "Or maybe overalls."

"Are you giving up expando-pants?" asked Meg. "Your maternity pants for men?" She was referring to my predilection for wearing slacks and chinos with a built-in three-inch expandable waistline.

"No way!" I said. "Once you go expando, you never go back. I'm just thinking of adding suspenders to the mix."

"How proud you must be," Cynthia said to Meg.

"I guess that yoga pants with suspenders might be a good look for him," Meg said.

"Hey," said Pete. "Kimmy Jo's teaching that class, right?"

"Hmm," said Cynthia warily. "Maybe."

Pete didn't know anything about Pilates, but looked thoughtful as he considered many of the yoga positions he was aware of, positions he mostly remembered from the strip clubs of his youth: the downward dog, the happy baby, the twisted half-squid, and the one-legged tree frog on a pole.

"He does know this is an exercise class, right?" asked Meg.

"I'm in," Pete decided suddenly. "At least till I snap my spine like a twig. Now, how about these murders? All wrapped up?"

"I'm happy to elucidate," I said, "but supper is ready. Pete, you pour the wine."

We sat around the kitchen table, passed the food around and made smacking sounds amid glowing comments about the cuisine.

"Delicious!" said Cynthia.

"Mmm," Pete agreed.

"It is very good," said Meg. "I'm glad to know that you are such a good cook."

"I've been cooking for years," I said.

"Bratwurst, hamburgers, steaks, and ribs," said Meg.

"The four major food groups," said Pete.

"The salad came from the Ginger Cat, the bread from Bun in the Oven Bakery, the wine from Bud," I said. "I did cook the lamb chops, though."

"And a fine job you did," said Pete. "The mint jelly is an especially delectable touch. Now ... murders."

I took a sip of the wine and could almost taste the bitterness of the unappreciated birthday clown's tears.

"Here's what happened. It was a Monday morning, and all the Friends-of-Ducks showed up to protest your inhumane treatment of the web-footed population of Sterling Park."

"Whatever," said Pete, waving off the criticism. "We solved the duck problem and made a few bucks on the side."

"I recognized one of the protesters, a girl named Bonnie Pickering. I'd gone to school with her as an undergraduate. We'd even dated for about a month. I hadn't seen her for thirty-five years, yet there she was. She denied being Bonnie Pickering, but she was lying. I saw it and Nancy saw it. Here's the thing. She and the first victim, Sabrina Bodkin ..."

"The trashy strumpet," said Meg.

"Yes, the trashy strumpet," I said. "They were sisters. Kent Murphee surmised it, and the DNA test confirmed it, but we didn't recognize Sabrina from the birthing classes, what with her insulated coveralls, hat and scarf. One of the Friends-of-Ducks, Coogan Kilgore, demanded that they all be in town for the protest, so Sabrina and Bonnie had to show up. They never thought they'd be recognized."

"Why'd they have to show up?" asked Cynthia.

"They didn't want to get tossed out of the group. Not just yet. They were running a fraud scheme on the rich guy, Halbert Grayson. Sabrina had stolen all his information and his identity. They were blackmailing Ellie Darnell for fleeing a homicide rap back in the '80s. Coogan and Cindibeth Lee were the only ones not being targeted, but I suspect Cindibeth would have been next. Also on the blackmail list was Bert Coley, and probably a lawyer in Boone named Jared Fish. Sabrina had affairs with both of them during the childbirth classes."

"What a pair of nasties," said Cynthia.

"They were all there on that Monday morning. Well, everyone except Jared Fish."

"And we fed them pancakes," said Pete.

"Gluten-free pancakes," I said.

"But we don't serve gluten-free pancakes," said Pete.

"But you *told* them they were gluten-free," I said.

"Well, I was a bit put out," admitted Pete. "Those duck people were jerks. I might have exaggerated the gluten-free part."

"Right. Then Sabrina Bodkin ..."

"The dirty harlot," said Meg.

"The dirty harlot," I said, "went back to her car right after eating, but she was severely allergic to gluten. She passed out."

"She might have slept it off," said Pete, "waking up with little more than a headache."

"Sure," I said. "We'll go with that. But someone spotted her car, specifically a telltale Mildred the Bear sticker on the back bumper, and knew whose car that was. They remembered it from years ago. That someone, or someones, as it turned out, also had a grudge to settle with these two sisters."

"And those someones were?" asked Cynthia.

"Angelique Murray and Christy Maze."

"Our postal clerks?" Cynthia was shocked.

"The very same," I said. "One of them saw the sticker, looked closer, and realized who was slumped over the steering wheel. Then one of them opened the back door of the car, climbed in, tied a quick knot with the rubber umbilical cord, and that was that."

"But you haven't arrested them yet," said Pete. "I just talked to them this morning over at the P.O."

"Sadly, we have no evidence. There are no fingerprints since it was freezing out and whoever did it was wearing gloves. There's no DNA that we can come up with, since Madam X was probably clothed head to toe in winter gear. Not a hair nor follicle that isn't Sabrina's or Bonnie's. Angelique's alibi is Christy, Christy's alibi is Angelique. They both swear that neither of them left the building all morning."

"What about the fact that Sabrina was blackmailing them?" asked Cynthia.

"Ah," I said, holding up a finger, "but she wasn't. Neither was Bonnie. It was a different hustle. They'd stolen the postal workers' identities back about five years ago when Bonnie was working at the post office, and nearly ruined them both. Both Angelique and Christy went through all the proper channels, reported it to the police, the postal service, anyone who would listen. Nothing was done, but the entire incident is well documented."

"So Sabrina ..." said Cynthia.

"The slutty tart," said Meg.

"The slutty tart," continued Cynthia, "met her demise at the end of an umbilical cord."

"She did," I said.

"Hang on," said Cynthia. "Are you going to let Angelique and Christy get away with it?"

"I'm not even entirely sure they did it. Just pretty sure. Besides, there's always new evidence that comes to light. There's no Statute of Limitations on murder. Now, how about that cheesecake?"

"Not yet," said Pete. "You didn't tell us about Bonnie Pickering getting run down like a groundhog on Mother's Day."

"Nothing simpler," I said. "When Sabrina was killed, Bonnie Pickering panicked, then decided to pack it up and move on. She didn't want to nickel and dime Ellie any longer. She wanted ten thousand bucks, and she wanted it quickly. Ellie didn't have it, and really had no way to get it, but she told Bonnie that she had the cash at her house, and got her to get in her Subaru. When they were on Old Chambers, she pulled her gun and told her to get out and walk."

"Then, pow!" said Pete. "Bounced her like a rubber ball."

"You could say that," I said. "Coogan found the banged-up car in the barn when the Ladies of BLaM showed up, and Ellie shot him hoping he hadn't spilled the beans. He hadn't, but we figured it out and we found the car. Ellie's in jail."

"How is Coogan doing?" asked Meg.

"Still in a coma, but the doctors say he's stable."

"Well, that's that," said Cynthia.

"That's that," I agreed. "Cheesecake anyone?"

"Wait just a minute," said Meg. "That's not that! What about the other murder?"

"What other murder?" asked Pete.

"Yeah," I said. "What other murder?"

"The murder of Father Jim, of course."

"*What*?" said Cynthia.

"*What*?" said Pete.

"*Holy smokes*," I said.

Chapter 27

Sunday morning broke frigid and gray, and it was apparent to anyone who'd lived in the mountains for any length of time that snow was imminent, and not just a dusting either. A cascade, a profusion, a blizzard, an avalanche, the end of civilization as we knew it — that's what we were looking at if indications could be believed. If you listened to the weather reports, we were all doomed. It was the Snowpocalypse. But really, who listens to weather reports? So Meg and I made sure Baxter had enough food for a few days, that the owls were taken care of, then hopped into the truck and headed to town to celebrate, with our friends, this First Sunday in Lent.

We arrived early enough to grab some coffee in the parish hall, then headed on up to the choir loft for what I knew would be a chaotic and quick rehearsal, everyone having to figure out how this Great Litany in Procession was going to work. I wasn't worried. We'd march around the church, or we wouldn't, and we'd chant, or we wouldn't. And then we'd go out to lunch and hopefully make it back home before the snows came in.

I looked over the bulletin, then opened a prayer book, found the service, and realized we'd made a mistake. Morning Prayer was a service of prayers and scriptures, and, although the Great Litany could certainly be included, it was to be included later in the service. We had it scheduled right at the beginning. Ah, well, I thought. Too late now.

The members of the choir came up the stairs, one at a time, and found their seats. They were already in their robes and surplices, and had their folders firmly in hand. When they were all assembled, I announced the changes to our usual Eucharistic service and explained the situation.

"What do you mean, no communion?" said Goldi Fawn.

"We have no priest," I said. "You have to have an ordained priest to celebrate a Eucharist."

"What?"

"Back in the old days," said Marjorie, "we did Morning Prayer three times a month. We didn't have communion but on the first Sunday."

"Really?" asked Rebecca.

"It's true," I said. "I remember those days. Anyway, since we had no time to rehearse, all the canticles will be spoken. We can sing the Psalm, and then sing the Parry piece at the offertory."

"No Kyrie?" said Tiff. "No service music?"

"Not this morning. We have the Great Litany, then prayers, canticles, and readings. Then the anthem, then a hymn. Next week, we'll have a better idea of what we're up against, clergy-wise. Today, well ..."

"Let's do it," said Bullet. His hair had gone from white to purple since we were in the season of Lent. He'd still be easy to follow.

We sang through the anthem and the choir had no real problems other than forgetting everything we'd worked on in rehearsal. It didn't take long to get it back up to snuff, though, and we had finished by the time everyone else was lining up for the procession. I sent the choir down to the narthex with their instructions. I had to play the prelude and then I could take a few minutes off. Bob Solomon and Mark Wells hung back, Bob, to run the sound system, Mark, because his hip was hurting and he didn't feel like marching around the church.

Georgia got up to the pulpit and made some announcements, mainly explaining that our priest had passed away on Thursday. This, for the few people who somehow hadn't heard about the tragedy. She commented on the Morning Prayer service and told the congregation that things would be back to normal as quickly as possible. It wouldn't be a problem. The congregation would just follow along in their prayerbooks like the good Episcopalians they were: standing, sitting, kneeling, bowing, a genuflect here, an obeisance there. Sing the hymns lustily and with good courage, as Charles Wesley advised.

Georgia took her seat in the front pew and Baylee Trimble got up.

"I know that we're all heartbroken for Father Jim's family," she said, "and of course, they're in our thoughts and prayers." She bowed her head and seemed to be saying a silent prayer, although her lips were moving. Then, that done, she looked up and said happily, "We have several classes available during this season of Lent, and I invite you to sign up for one of these offerings. We'll have sign-up sheets available in the parish hall during the coffee hour after the service."

She looked at a piece of paper that she'd brought with her to the lectern. "I'd just like to fill you in on some of our classes so you can be thinking about them. First, we have *Scripture Cookies Made Easy*, being led by Susan Clark. Then, my friend Candy Waddle is offering a seminar, *Lose Forty Pounds the Yah-Way*. This is a Christian guide to weight loss, so y'all bring your Bibles. Then we have a Bethany Moose Bible Study for women. And, oh yes, one more thing ..."

She yielded the podium to Kimmy Jo Jameson. Kimmy got up and dropped what appeared to be some sort of yoga inspired overdress to reveal her full figure clad in purple stretch pants and a lavender Spandex-Lycra top. Her top was sporting her logo: a man in a toga attempting some sort of activity that would get him arrested in most states. There were a few gasps from the congregation, women mostly.

"I want to invite all y'all to my exercise class," she said. "It's called *Paunches Pilates*, and it's for all you out there that would like to get in better shape. I will guarantee you results. Now, I know what y'all are thinking. 'Is there anything in this here Pilates class to alarm Bible-believing Christians?'"

"That's not what I was thinking," said Mark Wells.

"Me, neither," said Bob Solomon.

Kimmy Jo continued. "All Christians should be concerned with proper diet and exercise so that our bodies, which are the temple of the Holy Spirit, are kept in as good condition as possible. Y'all know that your body is a temple of the Holy Spirit within you, whom you have from God, right? You are not your own, for you were bought with a price. So glorify God in your body. That's First Corinthians six, nineteen and twenty."

Kimmy Jo gave the congregation a hundred watt smile. "So come and sign up after church. Y'all won't be sorry." She made a backwards sign of a cross as a nod toward our Episcopalianism, then reached down and retrieved her robe thingy and flounced off in the direction of the sacristy.

I looked at Georgia. Her head was in her hands, yet again, so I began to play, the *Organ Prelude on Rhosymedre* by Ralph Vaughan Williams. As I played, I could feel the tension leaving the space as the music filled the room. The power of music, as far as I was concerned, lay in its capacity to relax the spirit and open both our minds and bodies to that healing that God can offer. I'd seen it, and experienced it myself, many times. This was a long prelude, almost six minutes, but when it was over, there was a new breath settling on the congregation.

Finishing up, I spun around on the bench and saw, to my surprise, Meg. She hadn't gone down for the Great Litany and was looking at me with an expression I hadn't seen before. Not panic, exactly, but certainly not blissful contentment.

"What's up?" I asked, but then heard the first bell and the procession began. The congregation got noisily to their feet.

"O God the Father, Creator of heaven and earth," chanted Bullet. He was fourth in line following Humphrey Brownlow (a teenager carrying the cross), Benny Dawkins, and his protégé, Addie Buss, both of whom were wielding smoking incense pots.

"Have mercy upon us," replied the choir from the back.

Benny began with a simple maneuver, *Zacchaeus in the Olive Tree*. Up went the thurible, the burning incense leaving its ethereal trail hanging in the air. Over the shoulder, once, twice, then half again, whirling in circles across the oaken floor yet never touching.

Addie had begun her circumvolutions as well. Her thurible was smaller than Benny's and the chains were shorter, but that didn't slow her down, not by a long shot. Benny was one of the foremost thurifers in the world, having won most of the major competitions over the last five years. Although St. Barnabas was his home church, he was in great demand as a premiere smoke jockey, and could generally be found in one of the great cathedrals on any given Sunday. When he was in town, though, he was happy for St. B's to partake of his gifts. Benny could wield his incense pot and make the clouds of incense come to life. Addie was not far behind.

"O God the Son, Redeemer of the world," sang Bullet, as he trailed the smoking thuribles.

"Have mercy upon us," replied the choir and the congregation echoed them. Although the responses to the petitions in the Great Litany were led by the choir, the entire congregation was encouraged to sing along. It only took them a few verses to get immersed in the flow.

Addie began a figure eight, spinning in front of Benny. Benny joined in and, for several moments, the pots became blurs as they moved in and out, a dance of fog and silver, and when it was done, the two virtuosos moved on, leaving an image in their wake: a likeness of Moses holding the Ten Commandments, stern, yet loving, strong and beloved of God, and we all felt it. Then Bullet marched right through the vaporous patriarch and he dissipated with a poof.

"O God the Holy Spirit, Sanctifier of the faithful."

"Have mercy upon us," answered the choir and congregation.

Bullet made the first turn at the steps and started to lead the procession across the front of the chancel, just as we'd rehearsed.

"O holy, blessed, and glorious Trinity, one God."

He marched boldly through a smoky depiction of the Battle of Jericho. The smoke billowed, the church bell rang again, the congregation answered in unison, "Have mercy upon us."

"Excuse us, but may we have your attention please!" came the announcement.

My eyes snapped from Bullet to the Gospel lectern.

"Hayden," hissed Meg in a harsh whisper.

I waved her off, looking down at the speaker. There, wearing acolyte robes they'd obviously purloined, were Rodell Pigue and Sammianne Coleman.

"We need to take this opportunity to speak to the congregation," said Rodell, leaning into the microphone, his voice thundering through the church. Bullet, not sure how to proceed, stopped chanting and walking, and the procession ground to a halt.

"Turn him down, will you?" said Mark Wells to Bob.

"Nope," said Bob. "I'll turn him off."

Rodell rapped on the microphone a few times, then, hearing no return tap from the loudspeakers, raised his voice further. "You can turn off the PA, but you cannot silence us!"

"Rodell," said Georgia, "just what the hell are you doing?"

"We read the charter," he said, and waved his sheaf of papers aloft. "A church service counts as a formal meeting and any member in good standing can bring up a matter of concern at any formal meeting of the assembled congregation. Says so right here."

"That thing was written in the 1800s," said Georgia from the processional line. "Back before we had manners."

"Don't matter," said Sammianne, crossing her arms in defiance. "It's in the charter."

"Where's Billy and the ushers?" demanded Georgia looking around. "Get those two idiots out of here!"

"They all went for donuts," said Bev. "I believe their exact words were, 'We ain't stayin' in here for this whole danged procession. Let's go get us some donuts.'"

"I will kill ..."

"Now," said Rodell, interrupting her, "since this is an official meeting, we need to have a congregational vote on the church's policy concerning transgender bathrooms."

"We don't have a policy!" wailed Georgia.

"Exactly!" said Sammianne, her fist thumping on her palm. "We ... don't ... have ... no ... policy."

"Hayden," hissed Meg again, this time more urgently, but again I waved her off.

"What's a transformer bathroom?" asked a young kid from the middle of the congregation. His mother immediately picked him up and carried him out. Upon seeing this, a few of the other mothers followed suit.

"What about you, Mr. Pigeon?" said Sammianne. "You're running for the state senate. What's your views on this transgender bathroom issue?"

Jeff Pigeon was sitting in the third row. Now he stood up and turned around to face most of the congregation.

"Umm ..." he started.

"Yeah, Jeff," came a voice from the back. "What are your views?"

Jeff cleared his throat nervously. "Growing up as a young boy in Raleigh," he said, "where I spent my weekends delivering newspapers so that we could one day have an indoor outhouse, I never thought I'd be standing here, facing transgenderism in all its toiletized forms, or standing up against misgenderizing while remaining a highly regarded member of the chiropractic profession. But, my fellow St. Germainians, I *am* standing before you today, and for that, I am eternally grateful."

"Huh?" said Bob.

"Know this," Jeff continued with the full force of his convictions, "I believe in our Christian values and our right to bear arms. The empiricism of ecology is dreadfully doctrinal in its dual-sidedness while, at the same time, the complexity of bureaucracy is in reality quite independent of its sensibility. You see, we are here today at a crossroads. The issues we face aren't red or blue issues, they aren't transgender or antigender issues. They're America's issues. Thank you."

"Yes!" hollered the same voice from the back. "Jeff Pigeon for senator!"

"Well put!" said another, and Jeff was feted with a smattering of applause.

"What about our transgender bathroom policy?" whined Sammianne.

"We don't need a policy on transgender bathrooms," said Mark Wells from up in the choir loft. Heads all swung up in his direction. "But since you want one, here it is. All our bathrooms have one toilet and a lock on the door. That means a single-user at a time. They're *all* transgender bathrooms. Use any one you like. Men, women, Eskimos, unicorns: we don't care. Take your dog in. Take your grandma that used to be your grandpa in. Dance around in your skivvies! We don't care!"

More applause.

"Good enough?" he asked.

"Good enough," answered Georgia. "That's our policy. All in favor?"

"*Aye!*" came the resounding answer from the congregation.

"*Hayden!*" came an anguished voice from behind me. I turned to see Meg in distress. I know this because I've seen non-distress and this was not it. I moved over to her in an instant.

"My water broke about five minutes ago."

"*What?*" I was horrified.

Bullet, deciding that the moment had come for him to continue, resumed the march. The two thurifers had since departed, not being able to keep their pots afire, nor their artistry unsullied during such an interlude.

"Remember not, Lord Christ, our offenses," sang Bullet, his purple hair leading the way. "Nor the offenses of our forefathers; neither reward us according to our sins."

"Hayden!" Meg grunted, as the first true contraction hit. "She's coming!"

"Get down there and get some help!" I barked to Mark and Bob, and they were gone in a shot.

"Spare us, good Lord," chanted the choir and congregation.

The church bell rang again and Bullet made another turn. "From all evil and wickedness; from sin; from the crafts and assaults of the devil; and from everlasting damnation."

"Good Lord, deliver us."

I heard thundering footsteps on the stairs and turned to see Kimmy Jo, Goldi Fawn Birtwhistle, and Helen Pigeon, race into the choir loft.

"Oh, no!" I whispered, mostly to myself. "The ladies of BLaM."

"Don't you worry, Hon," said Kimmy Jo. "I used to be a nurse before I married Junior. That's how I met him. He was in a car crash and I was his bedside angel."

Kimmy Jo was still dressed in her purple Pilates outfit, and in a flash, she'd whipped her hair back into a ponytail and fastened it with an unseen rubber band. "Hot water," she demanded, "and plenty of towels!"

"We're in a choir loft!" I replied. "There's no water. No towels either. Marjorie's got a bottle of hooch in her hymnal rack, though."

"Hand it over," said Kimmy Jo.

"I've got some antiseptic hand soap," offered Helen.

"Hand that over, too," said Kimmy Jo. "Y'all scrub your hands."

They laid Meg on a couple of old robes that had been left hanging by the door to the belfry. Helen was behind her back propping her up. Goldi Fawn was rubbing her belly with some essential oils that she always managed to have handy, and Kimmy Jo was preparing to play catcher. Meg grunted in pain as a contraction hit.

"I'll be happy to life-coach you after this is all over," Goldi Fawn told Meg. "I'll give you a good deal. Three sessions for the price of two, and I'll throw in a free coloring."

"Uhhhhh," groaned Meg.

Helen pointed her gun finger at me and thumbed the trigger. "You might want to shoot that umbilical cord off with your roscoe," she said. "I saw that in a movie once when a copper delivered a baby but had nothing to cut the cord with."

"I got a styling wand," said Goldi Fawn. "We can clamp it off with that."

We heard Bullet's voice below us. "From all blindness of heart; from pride, vainglory, and hypocrisy; from envy, hatred, and malice; and from all want of charity."

"Go ahead and scream," Goldi Fawn said to Meg. "It's okay. I got you smeared up with this frankincense."

"I won't do it!" Meg forced out through clenched teeth.

"Good Lord, deliver us," answered the congregation. The church bell rang again, echoing through the building.

"She's embarrassed," Helen said to me. "Play something. Something loud."

"*Do it!*" yelled Meg, not able to contain herself any longer.

My fingers fell on the keys and I played for all I was worth, the organ opened all the way up, every stop engaged. I don't remember *what* I played. I think there was some Bach, maybe part of the *Great Prelude in C Minor*. Some hymn improvisations. I'm fairly sure I even managed to work in *I've got a joy, joy, joy, joy down in my heart*.

Meg yelled through the few contractions that were left and, although I never looked down at the congregation, I knew they were all staring up at the choir loft. Mark Wells had come back up and barred the door, while Bob had spread the word that there would soon be a new member of St. Barnabas. The congregation waited, and waited ... Meg's hollering stopped, the music stopped ... then, in the silence ...

"Waaaaaaaahhhhhh!"

Wild cheers and thunderous applause erupted in the building. I looked down and saw people embracing, bulletins tossed into the air, children being picked up and spun around in absolute glee. There was dancing in the aisles! Rodell Pigue grabbed Sammianne and gave her a huge kiss.

What could I do? My fingers found the keyboard again and since the organ was already at warp nine, I began to play, breaking Lenten injunctions that had stood for centuries.

Halleluia! Halleluia!

It was a postlude for the ages.

Postlude

Pedro and I made it out the sacristy door just as the church imploded, crashing to the ground in a fury of conflagratory extinguination.

"Well," wheezed Pedro, "that's St. Mumford-Pancake for you," referring to the fact that the real St. Mumford was flattened when a church fell on him, a bit of foreshadowing that probably should have been mentioned earlier in the story, but is apropos at this point anyway.

* * *

Meg and the baby were taken to the hospital in the ambulance just before the snowstorm hit. It hadn't been an especially difficult birth, and the two obstetricians on duty agreed that the three women who assisted did a fine job. Mother and daughter were both in great shape and came home a week later. They would have come home the next day, but there was no leaving the hospital once the storm hit and so all three of us spent a lovely week eating hospital food and watching bad home improvement shows on the television. Dave took his truck out to the house before the weather got too bad and picked up Baxter. The owls would be fine. I'd left a pile of frozen mice in the barn.

"I don't know," said Meg. "Do you think she looks like an Abigail?"

"It's hard for me to say. She sure is beautiful though."

"I don't think she does," decided Meg, then, "I think she looks like an Isabelle. Isabelle Rose."

"Perfect," I said.

* * *

"Tryxeeee!" I cried, sinking to my knees and ripping my shirt like Marlon Brando in the movie that time he was up for an Oscar — I could look it up on Wikipedia, but I don't have internet service right now.

"She's gone, pard," said Pedro, patting me on the shoulder. "She's gone to a better place, maybe Mitford or Bedford Falls."

"But the baby cows," I whimpered. "All those baby cows …"

"Yeah," said Pedro, "it's a shame. Now let's go get you a new shirt."

* * *

Father Jim's funeral took place in Florida, at the parish where he served for the last ten years. I went down for it, as did Georgia, Bev, and Mark Wells. It was quite a sendoff with a massed choir and a rash of bagpipes. Meg and Isabelle Rose decided not to go, staying instead with Ruby at her place. Jim's wife, Dorothy, played the grieving widow to perfection, but I did manage to catch the look on her face when she wasn't "on." Meg might be right, I thought.

Coogan Kilgore remained in a coma for one year, but then miraculously woke on the anniversary of the shooting. Upon regaining consciousness, he was presented with a hospital bill of $23,476,542.54 since he was found to be uninsured. He immediately moved to Canada.

* * *

"I'd like a new shirt," I said. "Not Lycra, though. I'm thinking something in a black linen. Maybe with a classic collar, a concealed front button placket, long sleeves, button cuffs, a box pleat detail to the back, and a curved hemline. You know, something classy."

"Tryxee would have loved it," said Pedro, "and you really have the shoulders to pull it off." He pointed across the street. "Plus, they're having an Imploding Church Sale at the St. Mumford-Pancake Gift and Shirt Shop. Twenty percent off."

* * *

The Lenten classes went off without a hitch. Pete and I signed up for *Paunches Pilates* and lasted one half of one session. We decided to take up golf, or maybe bowling. Meg and Cynthia stuck it out and were both breathtaking in swimsuits by St. Swithen's Day.

The church began its search for yet another priest, Georgia thinking that maybe this time we'd just let the bishop do it and we'd take what he gave us. It might work, she said, and I agreed. Either way, she was done being the Senior Warden when her term ran out. We had an interim priest assigned to us in just a couple of weeks, but that's a story for another time.

* * *

"Let's go shopping," I said, "then head over to Buxtehooters for some tuna casserole."

"Yeah, I need a drink," said Pedro. "Ermentrüde's touting this new stuff, 'Love in a Bottle.' Got a real kick, she says."

"Bark," agreed Rex the famous detecting dog, because a good writer never kills off all the animals in his story.

* * *

Bert Coley and Tiff St. James got married late in the summer, Tiff finally having the wedding she'd always dreamed of, except that she had a baby hanging on her breast, the wedding took place at the Bear and Brew on a Tuesday afternoon, Bert had gone squirrel hunting and was an hour late, the music was provided by Bullet who had learned the *Wedding March* on his new theremin, and both sets of her grandparents refused to come, instead attending a prayer vigil for her eternal soul. Other than that, it was her "Special Day." Bert began working for DigiZoot in March and, by the time they got married, he had saved enough to buy a house just outside of town. I didn't know if Bert had ever confessed to Tiff. I suspected that he had not. Tiff kept him on a tight leash.

Rodell Pigue and Sammianne Coleman got married as well. I did not attend the ceremony.

Dr. Neeraj Agrawal left Appalachian State the next year and eventually won the Turing Award, generally recognized as the highest distinction in computer science and the "Nobel Prize" of computing. He did not mention St. Germaine in his acceptance speech.

I never heard from Jared Fish's lawyer, although Nancy did see his "separation pending divorce" notification in the *Watauga Democrat* a few months later. Nancy was happy to visit his estranged wife and hand her some pertinent documents. Nancy was on "Team Linda."

Angelique and Christy continued working at the post office. We didn't say anything to the rest of the town and so, no one ever knew. Maybe we didn't know either.

* * *

And so, this tale ends as all good crime stories do: the case is solved, the detective makes it with the shapely dame, the jaded but ultimately soapy sidekick finds love in a bottle, the hero gets a new shirt. It was a dark and stormy night in the city that never sleeps and so is perpetually cranky. It's good to be a detective.

About the Author

Mark Schweizer lives in North Carolina where he pens the occasional mystery. He also composes choral music, and is vice president of St. James Music Press, a church music publishing company. You could look it up if you don't believe it. Really! www.sjmp.com

Donis is the president, but she gives him every other Thursday off to write his silly stories.

From the Author

If you've enjoyed this book — or any of the other mysteries in this series — please drop me a line. My e-mail address is mark@sjmp.com.

Also, don't forget to visit the website (sjmpbooks.com) for lots of fun stuff! You'll find the Hayden Konig blog, discounts on books, funny recordings, and "downloadable" music for many of the now-famous works mentioned in the Liturgical Mysteries including *The Pirate Eucharist, The Weasel Cantata, The Mouldy Cheese Madrigal, Elisha and the Two Bears, The Banjo Kyrie, Missa di Poli Woli Doodle, First Timothy,* and a lot more.